JESUS BUGS

NICHOLAS BRUNER

Other books by Nicholas Bruner

The Ballad of Dani and Eli
The Love Machine
Roll dem Bones

All books available at Amazon
(amazon.com/author/nicholasbruner)

Sign up for my mailing list and receive a free short story! **nicholasbruner.com/contact**

JESUS BUGS

NICHOLAS BRUNER

Jesus Bugs

ISBN 978-1-7354892-5-4

Cover design by MiblArt

This book is dedicated to Irene Strickland.

Preface

So Mizz Strickman told me it's bad form for a writer to put in a preface but screw that. I seen 'em in all those big books she has up on her shelves and it didn't hurt those books none. Anyway, following the rules ain't never done me no good. Not that breaking the rules has done me much better but at least it's my own choice. So here's the preface, like it or not.

I guess I should warn you my grammar ain't the greatest either. Now don't think it's because I don't know no better. I can read, but I always wonder why nobody ever writes in those books the way they really talk. Trying to show off, probably. Well, I ain't showing off. I'm just gonna put down exactly what happened, and I'm gonna write it exactly how I'd say it.

I'll start at the day of Big Joe's murder and put down everything that took place after that. If you don't care to read a book like that, I figure this preface should be enough to steer you somewhere else.

Foreword

Yep, I'm putting in a foreword too. Now in those books of Mizz Strickman's, they always thank all their editors and agents and best friend's girlfriend's poodle for helping them write their book. Well, I ain't got no one like that to thank. I only got Mizz Strickman and me. So that's who I'm thanking. If this book makes sense to you, it's probably 'cause Mizz Strickman went through and changed my bad spelling and all that. And if you like what I wrote, you can thank me, and no one else.

PART ONE

Chapter One

So like I said, everything started with Big Joe's murder. You ain't got to know too much about Big Joe, except he was pretty much the meanest mother to live in Wyattville, which is where I live, by the way. He lived in that nasty old house on Vance Street with his pack of slobbering coonhounds and he drank every day.

I knowed him cause his leg was lame and it was hard for him to get out, so he'd give me ten dollars to go down to the liquor store and pick him up the second smallest bottle of Old Kentucky Special whiskey. And they'd sell it to me at Jim's Liquors even though I'm eleven, cause they knowed it wasn't for me, but for Big Joe, and when I took it back to him he'd let me keep the change, which came out to two dollars and forty-six cents.

Now I guess Big Joe wasn't so bad in the morning, before the whiskey. He'd meet me at the gate and give me the money to pick up the bottle, and I'd talk with him a little, chew the fat, as some people say. And his dogs weren't so bad either since they knowed me, but they did slobber all the time.

But on this particular day—I remember it was the twentieth of June 'cause it was the day after school let out for the summer, and it's important I get this down exact—Big Joe wasn't waiting for me at his gate. When I stroll up, those dogs of his was all up on the chain link fence, whining and begging like no one had fed 'em. I was suspicious right away, 'cause you know, where's Big Joe gonna go with that leg of his? I opened the gate and slipped in, though I hated to let those dogs drool on me. And I walked through the yard, taking care not to step in any of the piles of dog shit.

I'll just come right out and tell you, the house was a god-awful mess. Furniture all knocked over and papers everywhere. I don't know how much of that was due to the murder, and how much it was already a mess from Big Joe, but I guess the blood wasn't there before. There was blood all over that living room, spattered across the back wall and the furniture where I suppose his guts landed after he was shot. I was thankful the dogs had not gotten in there.

I had to take a couple minutes to get ahold of myself. Don't get me wrong. It ain't the first time I seen a dead body. I saw Uncle Billy's dead body after he had his heart attack, but that was up at the funeral parlor and though his body had a smell, it was kind of a chemical smell, and he was laid out all nice in his coffin. But this was different. It smelled like Mama patting out hamburger patties, only real strong, and I knowed it wasn't hamburger patties but Big Joe's guts. I felt kind of sick in my stomach and I turned around to push that feeling down. And when I'd pushed it down, I forced myself to check, and sure enough, there was Big Joe's body, blasted clear behind his bloody couch, his big ole stomach full a holes, his fat face kind of frozen in a look of shock. I went over and closed his eyelids, like I seen in those crime movies Mama always watches, and that made me feel better.

I ran out of the house, but I didn't forget to close

the door behind me so the dogs wouldn't get in. I ran clear down to Jim's Liquors where Lynn was behind the counter and I blurted right out, "Somebody shot Big Joe."

"Oh my God," Lynn said. "Is he still alive?"

"Nope," I said. "He's dead, and his blood's all over the place up there."

"Oh my God," she said again. And she picked up the phone and called the sheriff. I wished she hadn't done that, but she did.

Chapter Two

I hated the Law ever since they sent Daddy away. I ain't seen him since I was eight years old, and I don't count it the two times a year when me and Mama and Robby drive up to the state prison in Neuse. When we'd see him there we got to sit at a table with him in a big cinderblock room and a bunch of other families visiting at the same time and the guards all standing around, and only got two hours, and no privacy. We could go every month, but we don't have the money to stay in a motel that often, and we don't know nobody in the area to stay with. So it's been three years and two months since I've really seen him. Well, what happened when the sheriff showed up at Big Joe's only made me hate the Law even more, if that's possible.

Of course I knowed they was coming after Lynn called it in, so I went up and waited in the woods near the house. She'd wanted to come up with me but she couldn't leave the store unattended. It took quite a while for 'em to show, but I learned later they stopped off at the liquor store first and Lynn told 'em what she knowed.

When I seen them pull up, I hid behind a stump so I could watch 'em. It was two cars, their flashing blue lights on but no sirens, and Sheriff Tate got out of one car and strode up to the gate. Of course the dogs ran right up—they was really frantic now, whether 'cause of hunger or 'cause they had a sense something was wrong, I don't know. But they was outdoing themselves, barking and snarling and practically throwing themselves against that high chain link fence, rattling it pretty good 'til I started to wonder if they might really be able to knock it down.

Sheriff Tate stood there a minute with his hands on his hips, his flabby belly pushing against the buttons of his uniform. To describe the look on his face I have to use one of those words I see in a book sometimes, but no one ever really uses when they talk, and that word is *contempt.* The contempt on his face was so thick you could've spread it on toast. And I guess he got tired of keeping that expression on his face, 'cause then he pulled the gun out of his holster and started firing into the pack of coonhounds. Not clean, one shot for each dog, but over and over, every bullet in the gun, like he was playing a video game or something. It was loud as anything I ever heard, and dogs was yelping and falling left and right, just staggering off into the yard and dropping, blood welling up out of their sides. And when he was done, the look on his face was different. The word I would use to describe it afterwards was *satisfaction.*

He had a problem, though, and that's that one dog had got away. I guess the dog had figgered the situation out and backed off, and it retreated around the back side of the house, whimpering. I believe Sheriff Tate was about to reload his gun when somebody shouted out, "Sir! We got a kid over here!"

And I whirled around about scared to death 'cause of course the voice was talking about me, and came from right behind me, and there was the deputy, walked right up and I probably hadn't heard him 'cause my ears was still ringing from the shots.

I ducked and took off but the deputy was too fast for me. I didn't get three steps before he had me by my shoulder, squeezing hard into my muscle with his hairy hand. And before I knowed it he had me standing right in front of the sheriff, with his fat greasy face and thick lips.

"You the kid who found the body?" Sheriff Tate asked me.

I glared at the man. I didn't have the inclination to speak to a dog-killer.

"He retarded or somethin'?" he said to the deputy.

"Don't know, sir."

Sheriff Tate squinted his eyes and stared up at the sun for a moment, then before I knowed what was happening he had the front of my t-shirt balled up in his fists, holding me close to his overstuffed face, a little puff of powdered sugar on his chin. "You look familiar to me. I reckon I seen you around somewhere." His breath stank like too much coffee.

"You don't know me." My heart may have been beating hard but I stared right back in his eyes and didn't blink.

"Maybe. Maybe not. But I sure as hell won't forget your face. Now tell me your name 'fore we give you a ride in the car."

"J.T."

"J.T. what?"

"J.T. Honeycutt."

Sheriff Tate grunted and let go of my shirt. He turned his head and stared at the house. Admiring his shooting, I guess.

"Deputy Snyder's gonna get your address in case we need to ask you anything else."

"You didn't ask me anything this time."

"Don't push your luck, son." He reloaded his gun and kicked the gate open with his booted foot. He went right in that yard, looking for the one that got away. I was *gratified* to see him step right in a big pile of what the dogs deposited all over that yard.

I gave the deputy the address 211 Pine Street, which is where this smartass at my school named Kevin lives. The phone number I gave him I made up right off the top of my head. Either the deputy didn't realize or didn't care and he told me to go on my way, so I did.

But now I got to admit I ain't been entirely straight with you. 'Cause I did maybe take a little something from Big Joe's house, before the sheriff got there, and that part I didn't mention to him or the deputy. Now I ain't talking about lying, so don't call me a liar. I just mean sometimes things are easier when you don't tell somebody what they ain't asked about, and he didn't ask, so I didn't tell him. Only I realize now, I got to tell you, or the rest of the story won't make sense. So yes, I did take something, and I'll tell what it is when I get to it.

Chapter Three

Big Joe didn't trust nobody. I was probably the closest thing he had to a friend and when we talked, it was all "how's your folks doin'" or "might get some rain today" or whatnot. So when he'd had a nip of whiskey early one day and got to telling me about this place in his bedroom with the loose floorboards, and how he got something down under there that a lot of folks were gonna want if they ever found out about it, I listened.

I didn't believe a word of it, but I didn't forget either.

And damn if it wasn't just like he said when I run up from the liquor store where Lynn was on the phone with the Law and I checked it out: the loose boards, and underneath a little leather bag that I slipped into the back of the waistband of my jeans. And when Sheriff Tate grabbed me by the shirt, I was shitting bricks that bag was gonna slip out, but it didn't.

No doubt they was gonna be looking for that bag. They might not think a kid like me already would have taken it, but when they searched the house and it was gone it wasn't gonna take them long to figure where it gone to. That's why, when Deputy Snyder told me to be on my way, I didn't wait around, but went straight to Rache's house. Rache would know what to do.

Me and her are cousins and almost exactly the same age. Mama and Aunt Marnie was pregnant together. Me and Rache knowed each other our whole lives. We used to be best friends, but we ain't no more. She been all stuck up lately, since her mama remarried rich. She don't wanna talk to me, she don't wanna be seen with me. Fine. I can take a hint. But she's also the smartest kid at school, and not just about books either. So I thought maybe she'd help me out just once, what with the situation I was in.

When I got to her house, her stepdad Laban was mowing the lawn on his Super Bronco lawn tractor, all shiny and red, wearing his khaki shorts and pressed t-shirt and breezer hat. Everything with him is just so—his trimmed yard, his vacuumed house, his crisp clothes, even his pretty wife. Everything but the obedient stepdaughter, but he's working on that. Anyway, he don't like me, but then, he wasn't going to see me. I snuck behind some azalea bushes and waited 'til he was mowing the other direction before I crossed to the house and knocked on Rache's window.

"J.T.! What the hell are you doing here?" Her face has freckles and her eyes are brown and her red-brown hair was tangled and she was the same as ever.

"I'm in big trouble, Rache. I need your help. I mean, I really need your help."

She leaned with her elbows on the windowsill and chewed her lip like she was trying to decide. Finally, she held her hand out so I could climb up over the sill and through the billowing curtains.

Rache don't have a pink room like some girls. Her walls are covered with basketball posters—Michael Jordan, J.R. Reid, Rick Fox—and she even has her own telephone shaped like a basketball. She's not just the smartest kid at school, she can outshoot and outdribble any boy in fifth grade. Her daddy used to follow

Carolina, so she's never taking those posters down. Even better is her stepdad is a Duke man, so it sticks in his craw every time he walks in there.

I explained everything to her as best I could. It wasn't until then I realized just how mixed up my mind was, 'cause I could hardly get everything out in a way that made sense.

"Whoa, slow down, J.T. Take a deep breath." She flopped back on her sky-blue bedspread. "So if Big Joe has this bag that's so special, why's somebody only shooting him now? I mean, he's lived in that house for years, right?"

"Yeah, I can't figger that either, but that must be the reason. Why else would someone want to shoot an old drunk like him, anyway?"

"Maybe he was mean to somebody and they got mad."

I shook my head. "Nobody's going to risk jail 'cause Big Joe slurred something dumb at 'em."

She popped back up. "Well, let's see that bag then."

I laid it on the bed. It was smooth leather, a little smaller than a lady's purse, thin and pretty heavy for its size.

"Aren't you going to open it?" she asked.

I studied her a bit out the corner of my eye. "I'm not sure I should."

"Why not? I thought we were friends."

She got me with that one. I hoped we were still friends. I unzipped the bag and shook out a manila envelope folded in half. It was all taped up, so I pulled out my pocketknife and sliced one end open. What spilled out wasn't what I expected. I guess I was hoping for diamonds, rubies, a big pile of cash. But it wasn't that. It was a bunch of black and white photographs, each one about the size of half a sheet of notebook paper.

Rache whistled low at seeing them and I couldn't blame her. Some of 'em showed folks on the street giving packages to people in cars, some of 'em showed men in suits smoking and sniffing drugs up their noses, and some of 'em showed grown-ups doing things I don't even want to tell you about—men and women, and men and men, and women and women. I recognized a few of the people, too—it was all of Wyattville's high and mighty. Sheriff Tate was in there, and Judge Satterfield who sent Daddy to Neuse, and there was Laban in a couple pictures too, in bed with somebody who was definitely not Aunt Marnie.

I glanced up at Rache and her eyes was fixed on those last pictures. I couldn't read her expression. Maybe it was shock. But we didn't get a chance to think about it because big footsteps came stomping down the hallway.

Damn it, I thought. I should've noticed when the mowing stopped. I grabbed the pictures and stuffed 'em in the bag and slipped real quick into the only hiding place I saw, Rache's half-open closet. She pushed it shut behind me.

Footsteps. "You getting your room clean?" came her stepdad's nasal voice.

"Almost done, Laban."

A foot tapped a couple times, I'm not sure whose. He hates it when she calls him his first name, instead of Daddy, which she won't never do. He must have decided to ignore it. "Good. And after that, you need to mop the sticky floor in the kitchen where you spilled your juice."

I guess she nodded or something. I don't know. "Did I hear you yapping in here?"

"I was talking to myself," Rache said.

"Uh-huh." Footsteps around the room. I was trying to stuff that leather bag back in my waistband without making a sound, but I must not have done too good a job, because the footsteps stopped right outside the closet, and the door slowly opened. I might as well been naked standing there, exposed as I felt. "Talking to yourself, huh?"

Rache's stepdad stared me down for about half a minute, and I matched him right back. Don't ever let nobody stare you down. He blinked first. A little bit of red climbed up his pasty cheeks.

"Nobody likes a liar, Rachel." Laban pointed a finger right in my chest. "As for you. Get lost, before I change my mind."

"Change your mind about what?"

"About the ass-whuppin' I decided you're not worth."

I was about to sass him back, but for once I had a smart thought in my head. *The bag, you moron. This is your chance to get out of here with the bag.* So I skipped out of their house, pretty relieved actually. I swung right back around below the open window to overhear, though that didn't matter too much. Her stepdad was in the middle of reaming her out, and he was *loud.*

"—told you once, I told you a hundred times to quit hanging around with that half-ni—"

"Don't you dare say it, Laban," Rache said.

"The point is, I said to quit hanging around with him. You got something stopping up your ears?"

"I did quit! I blew him off at school all year."

Well, that explained one thing.

"But you thought he'd be okay at our house?"

"He's my cousin. I have to help him."

I could practically feel the spittle flying out of his mouth. "I don't care if he's your goddamned long lost kid brother! I don't want him sitting his dirty ass on our furniture, I don't want him eating up our food, I don't want him in your closet rubbing up against your clothes, and I especially don't want him in your room putting his grimy little mitts on you. Got it?"

"Yeah."

"What's that?"

"Yes, sir."

But as he must have been going out, she said half under her breath, "He's your cousin too, though."

I could hear him whirl. “What did you say?”

“I said, he’s your cousin too.”

“Oh, no. He’s not my cousin, missy. That’s your mama’s side. Best decision she ever made was—”

But I guess we don’t get to find out what her mama’s best decision was because the telephone in Rache’s room rang and he answered right away. “Yeah, what is it? …It’s missing? …You’re fucking with me, right?”

It was right then I remembered something important. The job Rache’s stepdad had? The reason he had so much money for his house and clothes and fancy car and everything else? He was some kind of bigshot lawyer, some kind of initials. P.A. or something like that, and I knowed he was in tight with the sheriff and all them. His next words turned the hot day ice cold.

“You think a kid took it? Who? …The Honeycutt kid?” A long pause. “Yeah. I saw him just now actually.”

Believe me, I didn’t wait around to hear the rest of that conversation. I lit out like Rusty at the Charlotte Motor Speedway, headed to the piney woods where no grown-up with a pressed t-shirt was gonna go. When I reached a real deep part in the trees I stopped, my lungs and throat all on fire from running so hard. I put my hands on my knees to get my breath back.

At that point, I was feeling pretty low. Rache couldn't help me, even if she wanted to. Nobody could help me. It was the whole damn world against J.T.

Just like usual.

I had to run away, I knowed that. Didn't know where, just had to leave Wyattville. I could start walking and work it out on the way. My plan was to hit my house first, pick up a couple things from my room, and tell Mama I was spending the night with a buddy so she wouldn't fret when I didn't show later.

I was almost home when I had a suspicion, and stopped right at the edge of the tree line. My little brother Robby was riding his Big Wheel up and down the driveway, getting his speed up as he went down and hitting the brakes so he spun out at the bottom. A neighbor was out weed-whacking, a few birds in the background. Seemed quiet, but I wasn't fooled.

Yep, there it was. A cop car at the end of the street, parked in the grass as if that would hide him. Guess my little trick with the phony address didn't work. I hoped they didn't shoot Kevin's dog.

I wanted real bad to go over and hug Robby goodbye, and I knowed Mama would worry herself raw where I gotten off to. But there was no help for it. I could see the deputy in the driver's seat, and there wasn't no way I could've made it. So I turned back into the woods and tromped off to one last place I still might be safe, for a while at least.

Chapter Four

"Granny?" I opened the screen door of her trailer and poked my head in. "Granny, it's me, J.T."

"J.T. who?"

"Granny, come on."

She laughed, and it faded into a wheeze and ended in a wet cough. "Well, come in then, stop standin' there with the screen door open. You bring something for me?"

I stepped into her trailer with all the blinds closed, dust motes floating thick in the sharp planes of light shining around the edges. The little TV played *Days of Our Lives* with the volume too loud. I dropped a pack of Marlboro Reds on the table next to where she sat in her easy chair in her housecoat and house shoes.

"Good boy," she said without looking up from her soap opera. "What's got you lookin' so mopey?"

"I got to go, Granny. You'll probably never see me again."

She took the pack and thumped the end of it against her knee a couple times. "Now why do you say that?"

"I got somethin' some big men want. And they aim to get it back."

"You mean you stole it." That laugh again, wheeze, cough. She was so *frail.* I guess I never thought about it before. Granny was always just old to me, that's all. But standing there, my eyes adjusted to the dim, I could see how thin her skin was, like paper hanging over dry old bones. Strange thing, the last time I'd probably ever see her was the first time I'd ever really looked at her.

"I didn't steal it."

"Does it belong to you?"

"No, but it don't belong to them neither."

"So give it back to who it does belong to."

"He's dead."

Granny looked up from her soap opera at that. She

slowly leaned forward and screwed the volume knob down. Her watery blue eyes searched my face. "I don't know what this is all about, J.T., or why you dancin' around the facts. And I got a feelin' I don't want to know."

I opened my mouth to say something, but she held up one gnarled old finger to stop me.

"If there's some big men want what you have, you best think long and hard about givin' it to 'em. Now, don't tell me what it is. Just answer me this: why do you need it so bad?"

"I don't. But I ain't giving nothin' to dog killers like them."

"Fair enough." Granny peeled back the foil wrapping of the Marlboros, tapped one out, and lit it with a lighter from the pocket in her housecoat. She sucked that first puff in like it was the only reason she was still alive and exhaled slowly, talking through the smoke. "Don't get me wrong, J.T. The Lord says it's wrong to steal. But if a hungry man steal an apple, the Lord'll look the other way, 'cause he didn't put you here to starve. You understand me?"

Tears came to my eyes. "I think so. I'm not sure,

Granny." My voice broke at that last word.

She pointed at me with the glowing end of her cigarette. "Uh-uh. You can stand there and carry on all you want, but that don't get you nothin' but a cry-cry."

I wiped my eyes on my sleeve and took a shuddering breath.

"Good." She blew out a long stream of smoke. "It sounds to me like you mixed up in some bad business. Well, you old enough to get mixed up in it, you old enough to be a man about it."

"I don't know if I know how to be a man, Granny."

"Listen, J.T. If you got your mind made up you ain't returnin' what these men want, and you need to leave town, you do it. No more dawdlin' or bawlin'. You ain't got time for that nonsense. You hearin' me, boy?"

"Yes, ma'am."

"Now come give me a hug before you go."

I wrapped my arms around her, and she wrapped her bone-skinny arms around me, and I thought how somebody else doing that might break her in half, but I was careful.

There was a knock at the door, and Rache's voice

came in. "Granny? Is J.T. in there?"

"Well, now. It's a banner day in Country View Acres, ain't it? Two of my grandbabies visitin' at the same time. Come on in, girl."

Rache pulled the screen door open. She had a big camping backpack on and a sleeping bag in each hand. She put the sleeping bags down on the top step and stepped in. She smiled when she saw me. "I thought I'd find you here."

Granny clicked her tongue. "Don't tell me you mixed up in J.T.'s bad business, too?"

"I'm afraid so," Rache said.

"I expected you, of all people, would've had better sense than that." Laugh, wheeze, cough.

I was feeling pretty relieved right around then, knowing Rache was on my side. And that we was friends again, I hoped. I pointed at the sleeping bags. "So you think we should camp out in the woods?"

"Hold it." Granny held up a hand. "If there's a dead man wrapped up in this, the Law gonna be down here to talk to me. And I want to be able to tell them truthful I don't got no idea where y'all kids went. So y'all need to make your plans elsewhere." She stubbed her cigarette out in an ashtray. "I reckon y'all shouldn't stop in and see your mamas before headin' out, so give me your hugs and kisses and I'll pass 'em on."

We did and Rache slung her backpack on and I hefted the sleeping bags and followed.

"You two take care of each other now," Granny called after us.

"We will," Rache yelled back, letting the screen door slam.

The trailers on their concrete pads lined up in rows along the gravel lanes. Cars and semis whooshed past on Highway Seven-Oh-One. "You know we can't go on no roads," I said to Rache.

"That's why I'm not taking us on any."

And she was right, she steered us into the pines. The whooshing cars gradually fell away and all the sound that remained were birds singing and our footsteps in the pine straw.

"So what, we just go 'til we hit some grassy spot and camp?"

"No. I have a better plan than that."

The string tied around the sleeping bags was

digging ruts into my fingers. "Where are we headed then? Is it far?"

"You'll find out when we get there."

I sighed and tried to shift my grip on the bags. My stomach growled and I realized it was almost dinner and I hadn't eaten since breakfast. "Is it someplace with food?"

Rache clicked her tongue. "I'll tell you one thing, J.T. All your damn questions sure aren't helping us go any faster."

Chapter Five

The rocky road ice cream was cold, sweet, and chocolatey. I'd never had that flavor before, and I stuffed my face with spoonful after spoonful, digging into the rough part of the ice cream and leaving a smooth pit behind.

"C'mon, save some for me!" Rache yelled from her end of the longest couch I'd ever sat on.

I tossed the tub to her, spoon jammed in, and she caught it smooth as a wrap-around-pass. She threw back a giant bag of Ruffles, but I caught it by the bottom and half the chips flew out and skidded across the floor. So what? I ignored the full signal my stomach was sending and stuffed a greasy handful of chips in my mouth, washing 'em down with root beer.

My guts let out a gurgling noise so I dropped the bag to the floor and leaned back on a cushion, brushing off potato chip specks from my t-shirt.

I guess we'd made a pretty righteous mess. Crumbs and candy wrappers and soda cans everywhere. Little towers of Oreos rose on the coffee table among the drips of spilled onion dip. Why little towers? 'Cause I like to screw 'em open and lick out the frosting and stack the cookies on expensive furniture, that's why. It was like Oreo City up there.

Now at my house, you can see the foam in the couch cushions through where the fabric is thin, but this couch was brown leather and smelled like a baseball mitt. And that's not all. There was thick rugs and oil paintings of little villages in Italy or someplace, and shelves and shelves full of fancy-looking books. Just for show though. I opened a couple and their spines cracked like it was the first time anybody ever looked in 'em. That's how come I didn't feel bad about trashing the place. The owners of this house didn't really give a crap, everything just had to look right.

"Your uncle must be a millionaire," I said, rolling around on that brown leather so soft it felt like a kitten's fur against my skin.

"Why do you say that?" Rache asked.

"The couch. All the food. And look at the view." The big old window was wide as the whole wall, and outside was the Black River, as pretty as could be with a little wooden boat slip in the water, trees hung with Spanish moss all around, and their reflections shivery on the water's surface.

"Yeah, but he's not my uncle." She scooped out a big spoonful of rocky road and licked it around the edge. She didn't care I'd already had the spoon in my mouth. "He's Laban's brother."

"I guess he got money though."

"Sure. He's a lawyer, like Laban."

"Wait a minute." I took another sip of root beer. "No. You're wrong. If he's Laban's brother, that makes him your uncle."

Rache leaped from her end of the couch and before I knew what was happening she had me doubled over with a gut punch that knocked me to the hardwood floor and forced out my wind in a big gasp. All those chips and ice cream and root beer came right up the back of my throat and I gulped to force 'em back down.

"Wha—"

She perched over me like a panther and put her face two inches from mine. "Don't forget this: He's not my uncle, 'cause Laban's not my daddy."

I nodded up at her. "I'll...remember...that...."

* * *

Did I already say the house was huge? Off that main room with the big window was a kitchen, all shiny steel and so big you could've parked an F-150 in it. Second floor had six bedrooms, every two having a bathroom in between 'em. Outside, dark wooden decks wrapped around everything.

Of course, if anybody dropped by, we didn't look like paying guests, what with the side window we'd shattered and climbed through. That's why once it started getting dark, we decided not to turn on any lights. I mean, I don't think the nearest neighbors was within a half-mile, but I knowed the Law was searching for me, and Rache's people was probably wondering where she'd gone to. Someone might think to take a look out here.

We picked a bedroom with a sliding glass door out to the deck and *formulated* a plan. We put Rache's backpack and the sleeping bags by the door. If either of us heard any cars pull up in the driveway, or any doors open, we'd grab 'em up, slowly slide that door open as quiet as we could, and sneak down the deck stairway.

After we brushed our teeth (count on Rache to think of packing an extra toothbrush for me) we laid back on the big bed. There was way too many pillows and I threw a bunch off my side but got the idea to swing one at Rache's head. She swung one right back and pretty soon we were having a real pillow fight. The weird square-shaped ones were too hard to hold onto, so soon we were using the regular pillows. It was hilarious, just bashing at each other like morons, and even funnier when Rache hit me with one upside the head and it split right in half, feathers everywhere. We fell back on the bed we was laughing so hard.

But when the sun went down we had to stop and actually try to go to sleep. Even exhausted as I was, I couldn't keep my eyes closed. Maybe all that chocolate and chips and Cokes and ice cream. Or maybe 'cause every time I closed my eyelids all I could see was dogs dropping to the ground with gunshot wounds. Anyways, I knowed Rache couldn't sleep either.

"Rache?"

"Yeah?" Her voice close to my ear in the dark.

"Why'd you come for me? At Granny's?" When she didn't say anything, I thought maybe she hadn't understood. "I mean, it would've been a lot easier for you to forget about me."

She tapped with a finger against the mattress and the taps echoed through the bed like cannon shots. "Those pictures in your leather bag?"

"Yeah. What about 'em?"

"We got to show 'em to somebody."

"We do?"

"I think I know who. A lady. She works for a newspaper. Friends with my stepdad, somehow. But real nice. She came to our house for dinner one night and treated me like a grown-up. She lives down in Wilmington."

"That's why you came back for me? 'Cause you want to show those dumb things to some lady?"

"Don't you see? We can take 'em down with those pictures. Laban and everybody." More cannon shots.

"He was pissed as hell, you know."

"Who? Laban?"

"After you left, he got a phone call. He went crazy after that. Said he was gonna kill you. Stalking around the yard looking for you. Shouting and cursing at everything. I was pretty scared."

I didn't really know what to say to that. But I guess it didn't matter, 'cause Rache went right on talking.

"And that's not all. He found the manila envelope in my room with the end cut open. I said I didn't know what it was from but he called me a liar. His face was all red. But the next thing he said, I knew he meant it, 'cause it wasn't loud. It was quiet. Said he should kill me even for speaking to you. Soon as he left in his car I packed up and went looking for you."

"Thanks for doing that," I said.

"Sure. No problem."

I hesitated a little to ask the next question. "Are we…friends again?"

"We always were."

"Oh," I said. "It didn't seem that way. At school."

"I was just trying to get along with him, at first.

He didn't want me hanging out with you, and I did what he asked. For Mama. So she could be happy. But I'm done with that now."

It was quiet in that room. And pretty warm. I was starting to get a little sleepy now and didn't say anything back.

"I hate him. I hate his guts. He tricked my mama into marrying him."

"You wouldn't know about this place," I murmured.

"What?"

"This place." I had to force my words into shape through the sleepiness. "If not for your stepdaddy, you wouldn't know about this place."

"Yeah, I guess." Tapping. "When we came out here last, we went canoeing."

"Mmm hmm."

Rache went on talking for a while. Her voice was nice, but I wasn't really paying attention. I only heard one last thing.

"That river out there went on and on." She might have said it or maybe it was in my dream. "It seems like we floated for hours, all peaceful. I wondered where you ended up if you just kept following the river all the way to the end...."

* * *

It felt like only a few minutes later when I opened my eyes again, but it was bright daylight. I had to blink my eyelids open, so much sun was stabbing in through the windows. I was confused at first, before I remembered where I was. Right about then, I heard a noise that made my guts go to stone. The worst noise I could've heard: a door slammed downstairs.

Chapter Six

"Wake up, Rache!" She was passed out next to me, laying with her mouth half open, a little string of drool down her cheek. I grabbed her shoulder and shook, whisper-shouting in her ear. "Wake up, there's somebody in the house!"

Her eyes snapped open. "Damn it!" She rolled off the bed and pulled on her tennis shoes. "We were supposed to leave when it was still dark!"

Now all kinds of doors were slamming, and a nasal voice called out from downstairs. "Rache? You here, baby girl?"

Laban.

"Somebody's with him," she muttered. "He never calls me that. He's showin' off."

I went to the window. On one side the sunlight

glinted off the river water. On the other, a brand-new black Cadillac Coupe de Ville in the driveway—Laban's car. Behind it, a pair of cop cars. And in the gravel driveway, Sheriff Tate and two deputies sipped coffee out of McDonald's cups and smoked cigarettes.

"Rache, the Law's outside. There's nowhere we can go." It occurred to me. We hadn't heard Aunt Marnie's voice. Why wasn't she here? Unless Laban and the sheriff didn't want her there to see whatever they planned to do to us.

The sheriff. Laban was one thing. We could handle him. But Sheriff Tate was something else. Think of what he done to those dogs that ain't never hurt him. Now imagine what he'd do to me, who had something he was looking for. And Rache, who'd helped me out. *Abetted,* as they say in Mama's crime movies. I automatically put my hand to the back of my waistband to make sure the leather bag was where it should be.

"Calm down, J.T.," Rache said. "Take a deep breath."

I realized I was shaking. *Get ahold of yourself.* She was right, we weren't caught yet. "Should we make a run for it?"

"Ssh." She sat on the floor with her shoes untied. She ran her hand through her hair, more tangled even than usual. Her face was screwed up so I knowed she was thinking. "Listen. Can you sneak down the back stairwell without the cops seeing you?"

"Maybe." I checked out the window again. The deputies were laughing about something. They were kind of far away, out in the driveway under a tree, and not looking at the house. The sheriff had disappeared, probably gone downstairs. "I think so."

"Okay. Take my backpack and the sleeping bags and head to the canoe."

"The canoe."

"At the dock, right? Like I showed you last night?"

"Yeah, I remember."

Footsteps coming up the stairs. Rache waved frantic at me to leave.

"What about you?" I said.

"I'll be there in a minute. Have it untied and ready to go."

"What are you going to do?"

"Buy us time."

I nodded and slid the sliding glass door open slow and quiet. She opened the bedroom door and ran out. I hesitated just a moment, to listen.

"Daddy!" she cried. When she spoke again, it was with a catch in her voice. "Daddy, I'm so glad you came."

"Rache? Are you okay? Did he touch you?"

I gritted my teeth 'cause I knowed how much that performance was paining her. *Don't waste it.* I tip-toed down the outside wooden staircase and across the gravel to the dock. Maybe somebody'd see me and maybe somebody wouldn't. It was the same as sneaking out of school. Move fast but quiet and don't look back.

I wasn't real familiar with boats, so I set the things down in the bottom of the canoe in the middle between the two benches and stepped careful in it so it didn't tip. Kind of floated around but it didn't get away from me. I got on my knees on the back bench and went to work on that big ole knotted up rope tying it to the dock. I couldn't pull it free. The rope was all frayed and slimy and didn't budge when I pulled at it.

I kept trying at it for a few minutes and all I got

for my trouble was a bloody fingernail. Besides that, where was Rache? Even worse, I could hear them deputies voices getting louder now. Maybe they'd finished their cigarettes and coffee. Or maybe they was looking for me. I didn't figger Rache would've told on me, but Laban or the sheriff might have seen through her trick.

Just when I was considering if I should dive in the water and swim for it, here comes Rache down the dock and hopped right in.

"Took you long enough," I said.

"Well, I had to explain to Laban and Sheriff Tate all about how you kidnapped me."

"WHAT?"

"What was I supposed to tell 'em? They think I'm in the bathroom now. So let's go."

"I can't get the knot untied."

"Are you shittin' me, J.T.?"

"I'm not! It's all slimy. I can't get a grip on it."

She breathed out hard. "Well, that bathroom story's not going to work for long."

Even as she spoke, the deputies voices got louder. They had to be about to come around the corner of the house.

Rache crowded beside me on the bench and started pulling at the knot herself, rocking the boat like a toy tugboat in a bathtub. "It's too bad you don't have your pocketknife."

I looked at her and my mouth fell open. "I'm a dumbass." I tapped my hand against my jeans pocket, and there it was. "I had my pocket knife the whole time."

Rache slapped her hand to her head. "Well, get it out!"

I did and there was the deputies round the corner, just strolling like Sunday morning and hadn't seen us yet. I sliced through the top few strands pretty easy but I had to saw at it after that. That rope must have been an inch thick, each strand springing back as I rocked the blade back and forth.

I knowed they was gonna look up and see us any second but there was a shout from inside the house. "Goddammit!" came Laban's voice, higher than most men's. "That lyin' little bitch!"

That distraction couldn't have happened at a better time. I kept rocking with that blade, getting a little deeper each time. The pressure I was applying with my fingers caused the blood to flow from my torn fingernail down my middle finger and across the back of my hand, but I wiped it off with my cheek.

"Hey! You there, stop!"

I glanced up. The deputies had spotted us.

PART TWO

Chapter Seven

The deputies sprinted down the gravel path, but it was right then my knife sliced through that last strand of rope and the canoe slid in the flow of the river like a socked foot going in an old tennis shoe. I almost lost my balance as we jerked away from the dock. The only thing kept me from falling overboard was Rache caught my shirtsleeve and yanked me down to the bench.

The deputies were at the dock but I guess with all their guns and walkie-talkies and handcuffs on their belts they didn't want to jump in. They was hollering up to the house and finally one of 'em ran back up. Too late. We was around a curve and lost sight of 'em at that point.

Me and Rache ducked down in the bottom of the boat, one of us at each end. The ride wasn't real fast or nothing, just kind of gliding along, with the branches and clouds against a blue sky going by overhead. I guess I'd thought a canoe would be made out of wood, but this one was actually some kind of hard gray plastic, with a flat plastic smell down there at the bottom, mixed with a little green algae water. Not the place you wanna stick your nose for a long time if you can help it, but we was scared enough to huddle down there.

When there wasn't no sounds after a long while I craned my neck around the backpack to try to see Rache and found myself staring at the sole of her tennis shoe. She had somehow flipped herself on her back and was staring up at the sky. "I don't think they're chasing us," I said. "I guess we got away."

"I guess we did," Rache said. She straightened and looked at my face. "You got blood on your cheek."

"Oh. That's from where I tore my fingernail and rubbed the blood off."

She licked her thumb and I flinched away 'cause I

knowed what was coming but I wasn't fast enough; she was daubing my cheek. "Don't move! I've gotta get it off!"

"Stop it! You ain't my mama!"

"Don't be such a baby!" Now she had her other hand holding my head still while she wiped my face clean. I glared at her and she smiled back all satisfied. Something occurred to her though and her smile disappeared. "Seems too easy."

I nodded. "It does, don't it? Shouldn't they be after us with motorboats or something? Or maybe they're waiting for us downstream?"

"Hmm." She leaned her head back on the bench and stared up at the sky for a few minutes before straightening up again. "Shit. The highway overpass."

Of course. They'd be able to spot anything going by on the river below. "How far is it?" I asked.

"I'm not sure. We've been in the boat, what, an hour? Can't be too far. We'll have to go around it."

"How?"

"How do you think? We'll carry the canoe."

I shook my head. "Nuh uh. No way. If they can see us from the overpass in the river, how are they not gonna notice us crossing the road with a boat on our heads? Plus, we're gonna carry your backpack and the sleeping bags at the same time?"

"Good point." Rache leaned back and tapped her head with her pointer finger. "Okay, I've got it. We'll need a distraction. Something to draw 'em away. A big noise."

"What, like firecrackers or something?"

"Maybe...."

"What if they got a call from a house nearby? Like an emergency call?"

Rache stared at me. "J.T., you're a genius."

My face got a little hot at that. I've been called a smart-ass plenty of times, but I don't recall nobody ever saying I was smart.

"Alright, don't let it go to your head." She closed her eyes and started figgering. "When we get near the overpass, you run off and find a house and call the cops, tell 'em we're there, then run back to the canoe. Since they'll think we aren't on the river, the cops should leave and we can go on our way."

"How come I gotta do it?"

"Your idea. You're a faster runner than me

anyways, right?"

"Now I know you're buttering me up." No boy in fifth grade could outrun Rache.

"Still your job."

We floated on. There was a couple paddles in the bottom of the boat we got out and used to steer, but we didn't do much more than stick 'em more in the water in case the splashes might alert anyone we was there. It turns out we could hear the cops on the overpass before it came in view, what with the crackle and static of walkie-talkies. One thing about the Law—it ain't quiet.

We steered in the shallow water behind some trees and underbrush in a little elbow in the river, peeking through to see the red and blue lights flashing on either side of the bridge.

"They ain't playing around," I whispered. "They got four cars out there—two at either end."

"Time to go do your stuff," Rache said.

My sphincter went tighter than a dill pickle at that. I don't know why the mission should be scarier than standing right there hardly out of sight of the cops, but it was. Rache could tell—she always can—and put a hand on my shoulder. "You got this, J.T," she whispered. It calmed me a bit and my breathing got smoother. Then she nodded and it was time.

I crept up the bank and into the woods parallel with the road. About a quarter mile down and I come across a white clapboard house. Now I started to puzzle. Should I knock on the door and ask to use the phone? What would I say? I almost turned around and went back to Rache, but then she'd know what a pussy I was. No matter what happened, I wouldn't be able to live with myself if she knowed that about me. So I forced my legs to take me to the back door.

I knocked pretty hard. Nobody came. I knocked louder. Still nobody. Around the front side of the house wasn't no cars in the driveway. I rang the front doorbell. A bob white bird called in the distance. "Bob White! Bob White!"

I hadn't thought about nobody being there, but actually that should make it easier. Just go in and use the phone. I tried the front door but it was locked. Back door too. What now? Go to the next house? But all I saw was trees. No telling how far to the next place.

No help for it then. I grabbed a heavy log from a woodpile by the garage and found a low window on the back porch. Did I really dare? I pictured a cop with binoculars spying the canoe and Rache beside it. Might be happening even now, all because I was diddling around here.

I took a deep breath and rammed it through the window. It bounced back, so I rammed it again, and this time the glass smashed. I hate to say it, but it felt kind of good turning that whole window into a thousand little pieces tinkling onto the floor. There was still shards all around the edges so I pushed 'em in with the end of the log and climbed through.

Inside was a bedroom, kind of musty. No phone, so I made my way to the kitchen. I could tell the place belonged to old people from the things lying around. Yellow old pictures in frames. Knick-knacks and gee-gaws and little crocheted pillows everywhere. I guess old people have all those knick-knacks 'cause after your whole life of getting 'em they start to pile up. I don't know why nobody ever throws any of that crap away, but they never do.

The kitchen was all faded linoleum and cleaned

dishes in a plastic drying rack. The phone turned out to be one of those old heavy black ones with a cord. It even had a dial for the numbers like in the movies. I felt like a private eye as I dialed the number and listened to the little clicks.

"Nine-one-one, what's your emergency?" A lady's voice, real business-like.

I tried to make my voice deeper, like a grown-up's. "Them kids that are missing? Um. The kids that was kidnapped. They're here. At my house." *Ugh, you sound like a dumbass.* I should've rehearsed a little before calling but too late now.

"Ma'am, do I understand there are kidnapped children at your house?"

Ma'am. At least she didn't think I was a kid. "Yeah. Yes. I mean, I didn't kidnap 'em. But they're here. The ones the cops are looking for."

"Okay. What's the location of the emergency, ma'am?"

"They're…on my front porch."

"Ma'am, what is the address of your house?"

The address? How should I know? "Um, they're getting away! I can see 'em running into the woods.

I'm going to go out and try to catch 'em."

"Ma'am, do not try to catch them. What is your address so I can send somebody immediately?"

"Um, okay, one second." I tried to think. What would Rache do? No time to run outside and check the number on the front of the house, and I didn't even know which street I was on, anyway. I looked frantically around the kitchen.

"Ma'am, are you still there?"

"Yeah, one second." Aha! On the counter, next to a can of salted peanuts, a big pile of bills. Perfect. "The address is 13523 Gorman Road."

"Thank you, ma'am. Where are the children now? Can you see them?"

I didn't know the answer to that and I'd given her the address. Why should I keep talking? I had to get back to the canoe. So I hung up. I turned and was about to go. The phone rang again.

I hesitated. Answer it? Was it the operator again? Probably. But what would I say to her? I let it ring and headed back down the hallway.

There was a closed door I hadn't gone in before and I could hear a phone ringing in there. And another noise too, like a moaning. I stopped outside and listened. There was definitely somebody in there. Or something.

I don't know why, 'cause Rache was waiting back at the canoe and the cops was on their way, but I just had to see. I reached out and turned that doorknob. I knowed it was stupid, but I did it anyway. Rache was wrong. I ain't no genius. Unless you mean a genius for finding trouble.

The shades was closed and it was pretty dark. A glass of water with teeth in it next to a blue box of Polident on a nightstand. A musty smell like in the first bedroom. A sort of mechanical breathing sound from the corner. I swiveled. In an easy chair sat an old man with tubes from his nose to a tank on the ground.

He stared up at me and made a sound. "Hnnn."

I froze. "Can…can I help you?"

"Hnnn." He had big ole quivering jowls hanging down from his cheeks and a tangled wisp of white hair on top of his head. He lifted an arm and stuck out a single shaking finger, pointing it at me. "Hnnn!"

"I'm sorry. I don't know what you want."

But I did know. That finger. Those eyes. He was

accusing me. He'd heard the shattered glass and the phone was still ringing, must've been about fifteen rings by now. He knowed it was my fault. And I felt ashamed. I'd been scared, but it was also *fun.* Breaking the glass, running through a strange house. But it wasn't a playhouse. Somebody lived here, somebody helpless, like Granny.

"I'm sorry," I said. I didn't know what else to say. "I got to go now."

I carefully closed his door again and climbed out the window I'd broken, avoiding the sharp edges, and it was only when I got outside I realized it would've been faster to simply go out the door. Another brilliant move by J.T. Honeycutt, Boy Genius.

Back at the river, it was obvious right away Rache's plan had worked 'cause the flashing lights was gone and so was the walkie-talkie static. Rache was leaned over right by the canoe and ready to shove off.

"They started pulling away about ten minutes ago," she said over her shoulder. "I think it's clear. Get in and let's go."

I did and she pushed us out in the water and I helped her step in with her dripping shoes. We paddled a little bit out into the flow but tried to stay close to the shore. To distract myself from looking up at the bridge I watched Rache instead. Wide eyes, her grip on the paddle so hard her knuckles was white. She was scared too.

But remember what I said about sneaking out of school? Move fast and quiet. Don't look back. And that's what we did as we floated right through the concrete posts. It was cool under the bridge and then warm again in the sun on the other side.

"We did it," Rache said when we'd gotten far enough to talk.

"Yeah, we did it," I said.

"What's the matter?" she asked. "Aren't you happy about getting away?"

"Sure," I said. But I wasn't sure. I wondered about that old man in the house, with his photos and knick-knacks and private eye phone. Did he have somebody to take care of him? A wife, or somebody else in his family? Who was gonna clean up that glass? I patted the leather bag in the back of my jeans. *It'd better be worth it.*

Chapter Eight

All morning long, we expected to see the sheriff or Laban along the shore any minue. Every time we came around a bend in the river, we froze, afraid they'd be there. Standing, waiting. Maybe a cop car, pulled up to the edge in some cleared area. We barely talked, and whispered when we did.

Hour after hour went by with no sign of the sheriff or Laban, or anybody. We started to relax and use normal voices and cupped our hands to bring cool river water up to wash our faces after sweating it out at the bottom of the canoe earlier. And of course, Rache talked a lot, like any girl. But I liked it when she did. She knowed a lot about everything around us, of course.

"Those trees with the trunks that spread out at the bottom and the big old branches are cypress," she was saying. "Those tall ones are loblolly pines. You know that one there with the rough bark, right? You got a lot of those in your yard."

I shook my head.

"Those are sweetgum trees. Drop those prickly brown balls."

"Oh, yeah. I use 'em as bombs for my army men." I dipped the tip of a paddle in the water and watched the streak it made, starting narrow but spreading wide behind us. "How do you know all that anyway?"

"Girl Scouts, some," she said. "But mainly from Mama. She can tell all about trees and birds. And herbs and things. I just listen."

A stick passed by us black and shiny in the water and she pointed at it. "Be careful with those. You think it's just a stick but you go to pick it up and it turns out to be a water moccasin."

"Yeah, Jackson at school, his older brother picked one up and it bit him and his skin turned all black and fell off. Jackson said it was pretty gross."

"Jackson's a liar," Rache said. "Don't believe what

he says."

"You don't think that's what happens if you get bit?"

She considered a minute. "Well, he's right about that. But I still think he made it up about his brother."

I nodded and dipped the paddle in again.

It was probably around noon when we decided to stop at a grassy flat spot along the bank and eat lunch. There was a forked tree trunk sticking straight up in the shallow water we could lodge the canoe in. We got our shoes and pant legs pretty wet trying to get out, but I didn't care, my legs was so tired from sitting all morning. Rache built a little wigwam out of sticks and I gathered up tinder and kindling, whatever the difference between those is, to stuff underneath. She got out some matches from her backpack.

She held a lit match at the bottom of the kindling and a curly little flame came up. We watched it twist a couple twigs with its bright heat but I was afraid it would die so I took a big handful of leaves and dropped it on, which nearly smoked us out.

"You tryin' to send smoke signals to the sheriff?" Rache rasped at me, and I couldn't answer her for choking myself, but when the leaves was all burned out, we did have a fire going. Rache got out her canteen and a little steel cooking pot from her pack and soon we had hot water for powdered eggs and hot chocolate. She only had one set of camping stuff, so I got the spoon and the bowl, and she got the fork and a plate. It didn't taste too bad. Afterwards we scrubbed it all out with soap and what was left of the hot water. I don't believe Rache forgot to pack a thing we might need in that backpack of hers.

"Back on the river?" I asked.

"Of course," Rache said. "Why wouldn't we?"

"Might be safer walking. Sheriff could be waiting for us downstream again."

She shook her head. "I think we threw him off the trail with our trick. Anyway, maybe we get caught either way. Wouldn't you rather ride than walk?"

I couldn't argue with that logic, so we got underway.

The afternoon was drowsy, little water sounds and insects singing from the shore, the canoe going in and out of sunny patches. Dragonflies buzzed loops in the air. Leaves reached down almost to the surface of the water like the trees themselves were drifting to sleep. I felt like we needed to wake up a little.

"Damn it!" I yelled out. My voice echoed real nice down the river.

"What'd you do that for?" Rache asked.

"Why not? Who's going to stop us?" I thought for a minute and yelled another one. "Donkey balls!"

Rache looked skeptical and I thought she'd get all superior, like she's not the cussingest girl in fifth grade. But she surprised me.

"Bastard!" Her eyes lit up as nobody answered her bad word. No parents, no teachers, no sheriffs. "Ooh."

"See, it's fun, right?" I said. "Horse shit!"

"Asswipe!

"Dick licker!"

"Shit ass!"

I gave Rache a look. Did I dare? I grabbed the sides of the boat with my hands and lifted my chin up so I could yell it extra loud. "Motherfucker!"

"You shouldn't have said that one," she said.

I grinned. "But I did."

"You're bad. I should've let you fall in back at the dock."

"You just ain't got the guts to do it yourself."

She checked around the canoe.

"There ain't nobody hiding behind a stump or nothing," I said. "Nobody but us for miles."

"I know that." She set her jaw. "Fuck you!"

"Pretty good," I said, but she wasn't done yet.

"Fuck you! Fuck you, Laban! Fuck you! Fuck you!" And then she screamed, closed her eyes and balled her hands into fists and pierced the air with the biggest, piercingest, shrillest scream I ever heard. I covered my ears but it couldn't keep that scream from burrowing through my fingers right into my brain. She kept going and going and I didn't know how she even had that much air in her lungs.

When she was done it was quiet. And I mean quiet. No birds. No insects. Even the river held its breath. The noises came back slow and when I raised my eyes her cheeks were wet.

I didn't speak for a while, and when I did my voice was small. "Are you okay?"

She nodded. "Better than I've been in a long time."

* * *

That night it was more powdered eggs and cocoa and figuring how to put up the tent, which got us good and sweaty before we managed to get all those poles and stakes and flaps where they're supposed to be, or close enough. But that wasn't even our biggest problem.

What to do about the canoe? No rope to tie it off, and we'd wedged it in a stump in the water like at lunch but that didn't seem like a permanent solution. Didn't want to risk waking up and finding it gone. The only thing to do was pull it up on land, except the shore here was ridgy, not low and sandy.

We got our shoes off and our pants too since this was going to be a major operation. Yep, we were in the river in our underwear, and I sure was glad the fifth grade wasn't there to see that. Now you might think the canoe would be pretty light 'cause it was plastic and not wood but you'd be wrong about that. We both got underneath the boat to push it up, feet sliding in that slippy, sucky river mud and we got it sort of up onto some roots so Rache climbed over and started pulling, and we eventually did get it onto dry land.

We were covered in sweat and mud and bruises

from that boat banging against us. Rache got out some cleaning wipes from her backpack and that's how we took a bath. An awful weird-smelling one, and I don't know that either of us really felt clean, but it's as close as we were going to get.

I guess it's true what they say about hard work making you sleep better 'cause as soon as I slipped in my sleeping bag, I was out.

* * *

I was lying groggy in the morning, snuggled down warm in my sleeping bag but a bit of nip on my nose, and wondering why everything inside the tent glistened like it was wet. I reached a finger out to the smooth material of the tent wall and a single water drop formed and rolled down my arm. From somewhere far away came a low rhythm, half vibration, half noise.

I wasn't even sure it was real at first. I listened hard, trying to capture it. It would stop and start again, and sometimes the beat would change. Indians? Some weird kind of machine? Surely no animal made a noise like that.

Rache rolled over on her back and her eyes were open.

“Do you hear that?” I asked.

She nodded.

“What do you think it is?”

“Drums,” Rache said. “Someone’s playing the drums.”

Chapter Nine

"C'mon, let's go see." I pulled on Rache's arm. The drums were driving me crazy, those rhythms bouncing through the trees.

"What about the tent? What about our gear?"

"We'll get 'em later. There's nobody out here but us. C'mon." I was practically dragging her by now.

As we got closer we could hear cymbals, toms, things I couldn't tell what they were. Soon a little house came into view. A real sad looking place. I mean, leaning over, almost falling apart actually, with shingles coming off the roof, bushes and weeds all overgrown. There was matted pine straw instead of a yard and a gravel pad instead of a driveway, but it didn't matter since there wasn't no car there anyway.

But there was a separate garage off to one side, and that's where those beautiful drums were coming from. The garage door was wide open, so Rache and I went up and stood underneath.

The man playing had his eyes closed. He had long gray hair down his back and no shirt on. I wished he did, though, 'cause except for the drums, I don't think he exercised too much. Flabby around the middle, a patch of scraggly gray hair on his chest, thin lines of sweat streaming down his pale skin. But man, was he playing those drums like anything. He was beating out whole rhythms that were songs by themselves, like he didn't need anyone on guitar or piano to play along with him.

A yellow dog lay on the floor whose head perked up when we walked in. He kept an eye on us but didn't bother getting up. We stood there and gawked at the drummer for probably ten minutes, his arms and legs working like a machine, almost too fast to follow as they flashed all over that drumkit. He stopped, suddenly, in the middle of a run and cocked his own head kind of funny.

"Who's there?" he said, and when he opened his

eyes I understood, 'cause the eyeballs was milky like a bowl of cereal.

"It's just two kids," Rache said. "We heard you playing and wanted to see."

"Yeah? Y'all like what you hear?" He stood up and grabbed a towel hanging from a nail on the garage wall and wiped the sweat from his face and chest.

"It was about the best thing I ever heard," I said.

"What's your dog's name?" Rache asked. "Can I pet him?"

"Go ahead'n pet him. I call him Here Boy."

Rache and I leaned over and patted and scratched him. His fur was coarse but he was warm and he stood and stretched out his front legs and leaned into our wiggly fingers.

"Here Boy's not much of a name," I said. Rache gave me an ugly look 'cause she thought I was being rude, but I can't help it. Sometimes the truth ain't pretty.

The man chuckled. "I guess not. But he don't seem to mind." The man held out his hand. "My name's Jerry, by the way."

Rache and I shook his hand and introduced

ourselves. I guess it was then my stomach realized it had nothing in it 'cause it let a growl, and I mean loud. I knowed Jerry heard it, too, 'cause the next thing he asked was, "You kids want some breakfast?"

"Anything but powdered eggs," I said.

"Oh, we got better'n that. C'mon into my palace."

Rache gave me another look, I supposed in case I had some smart comment on his house too, but I didn't have nothing to say on that subject. I only comment on things people can help if they got a mind to.

Jerry walked with a bit of a shuffle, not like his leg was hurt, but more like he wanted to make sure there was nothing in front of him. But he knowed where he was going even despite his vision.

When we got to the front door Jerry and Here Boy went in. Rache leaned over and whispered in my ear. "Are you crazy? We can't go in there. We hardly know this guy."

"He's blind. What's he gonna do to us? 'Sides, I'm hungry." I stepped in the front hall and glanced back. I could tell from her narrowed eyes she didn't like the situation but she followed me into that crooked house.

We sat at the kitchen table while Jerry made

everything. It was weird, 'cause I wouldn't say the house was clean, exactly, but everything seemed to have its certain place so Jerry could find it. And you wouldn't think a blind man could cook, either, but in just a few minutes he had a big steaming pan of eggs and ham that he was scraping off with a spatula onto some mismatched plates.

"This alright with y'all?" He slid plates in front of Rache and me and I wondered—how did he know where we were sitting at the table?

"It looks great," Rache said. "Could I get a glass of water?"

"Oh, sure." Jerry found a chipped glass in a cabinet and filled it with water off the tap. I had to laugh when he set it in front of Rache, though, 'cause that water was almost as yellow as the dog and had a little film at the top, and that frown on her face with that nasty water was too much.

"What's funny?" Jerry asked.

"It's the water," I said. "Is that how it comes out?"

"Well, now. You can tell I don't have kids visit too often. I don't drink the water myself. Why don't you look in the refrigerator? I think I got some Cokes in there."

I went over and opened the door. The refrigerator was stuffed to bursting with cans of Miller Genuine Draft. Oh, there were a few other items—the egg carton, a jar of pickles, mustard. But there must've been about two hundred cans of MGD in there. I scanned shelf by shelf. "I think I see a couple Mountain Dews at the back."

"Help yourselves."

I had to reach way back to get those Mountain Dews. Rache smiled at me when I handed one to her.

Jerry got himself a beer and sat at the table with us. He cracked it right open, didn't seem to matter it was breakfast time. "Anyway, I don't get too many folks out this way. What brings y'all out here?"

"We're on a camping trip," Rache said.

"By yourselves?" Jerry took a sip while neither of us said anything. "Your parents know y'all're out here?"

Still we didn't have nothing to say.

"I see," Jerry said. He traced his finger around the lip of the can. "Camping, huh? Y'all got tents and things?"

"We keep the tent rolled in the backpack," Rache said. "And we got two sleeping bags besides."

"Mmm-hmm." Jerry tilted his head. His white eyes was open and staring, though of course he couldn't really see nothing. I was afraid he was fixing to tell us to take a hike, and was only figgering how he could say it nice. So his next words was a surprise. "Okay. After breakfast, why don't y'all bring your camping gear up to the house and meet me at the garage? I got somethin' to show you."

* * *

It was a lot easier to pull the tent down than to put it up, but fitting all the stakes and flies and whatnot back in the tent bag was a hassle, especially since Rache wouldn't let me just stuff 'em in, but insisted everything be rolled up and packed right.

"Hold your horses, J.T. Let's do this the right way."

"Ugh," I exhaled. "Fine." We folded the corners of the tent together end to end, and then matched those corners up too, and so on 'til we'd made it a neat little square.

"What do you think of Jerry, anyway?" I asked.

"I think he's a nice man," Rache said. "But we should be moving on."

"Why? What's the rush? Let's stay here a while."

Rache placed the folded tent square on the ground and carefully kneaded the air pockets out with her knees and hands. "We've got to get those pictures to Wilmington. Before the sheriff finds us."

"I think we lost him at the overpass." I held the backpack while Rache worked the tent in there. I was all for Rache's plan, though I was having a hard time figuring out exactly what this friend was going to do with the pictures, or why we had to be in such a hurry about it. "Anyway, even if he's still after us, won't he be looking on the river? We're probably safer at Jerry's. He'd never to think to look for us there."

Rache closed all the flaps and adjusted the straps on the backpack, but didn't say anything.

"C'mon, Rache. At least let's see what he wants to show us."

"Okay." She put her arms through the backpack straps. "I guess we can take a little break. But as soon as he shows us, we're back in the canoe."

Chapter Ten

We found Jerry in the garage rummaging through a trunk in the corner. He pulled out a tambourine in one hand and a pretty big pair of bongos in his other. “Who wants this one?” He held out the tambourine.

“I do!” Rache took it from him and thumped it rattling against her leg.

“Sounds like you already know what to do with it,” Jerry said.

“Yep, we used tambourines at church camp.”

“Alrighty then. I guess you get these.” He handed me the pair of bongos. “How ’bout you, J.T.? You know what to do?”

“Sure, I just slap ’em and the noise comes out.”

“Well.” Jerry stroked his chin. “We’ll have to work

on it with you a little. Have a seat in that chair over there."

I sat in a wooden chair along the wall.

"Now set the bongos on your knees, little one over your left knee, and tap the skins with the top two-thirds of your fingers."

I did and it sounded pretty good.

"Okay, there you go," Jerry said. "No slapping, just fingers." He sat down at his drumkit and picked up the sticks from the snare. "Okay, let's get started on the count of four. One…two…three…four."

And Jerry was off, me and Rache trying to keep to the beat. It didn't sound half-bad, although I don't know how much we really added. But it was fun. We must have played a good thirty minutes there with Jerry. He kept his eyes closed and his head bobbing and he'd call out encouragement to us. "That's it! Shake that tambourine! Hit those bongos!"

I could've played all day, but Rache got bored after a while and sat with Here Boy on the garage floor, rubbing him up good. The sun was higher now too, and it was getting pretty roasting in the garage.

"Alright, break time," Jerry finally said, replacing

the sticks on the snare. "Let's walk into town and pick up some fishin' worms."

I hated to end the bongo session, but I was awful curious to see how Jerry made his way to town. I looked over at Rache. She shook her head and pointed with one finger towards the river. I nodded my head in agreement and pointed towards Jerry. "Do you need any help carryin' anything?" I asked him.

Jerry laughed. "No thank you. Just y'all's company is enough."

Rache gave me an exasperated shoulder raise with her palms up, but I won that round. It was off to town.

* * *

It turns out Jerry walked with sort of a cane. Not a wooden cane, but a long metal one that he swept from side to side on the ground in front of him to make sure nothing was in his way. He didn't walk real fast, but he wasn't too slow either. Here Boy came along too, trotting beside us with his tongue hanging out, happy as a dog could be.

It was about a mile along a gravel road to what

Jerry called town, which was really a handful of stores just off the highway. A liquor store, a Family Dollar, a second-hand clothes shop, and a restaurant with real Kountry Kooking. But our destination was Ed's Convenience-Groceries-Gas, with the coldest beer around and a dozen nightcrawlers for two dollars, according to the wooden signs in the windows.

An older man with a pair of reading glasses on the bridge of his nose sat on a stool behind the counter. He lifted his eyes without raising his head from his newspaper when the door chime rang. "How's it going, Jerry? You brought some visitors with you today, I see."

"Morning, Ed. Sure did. My niece and nephew."

"That's real nice," Ed said, going back to his paper.

"Why don't you two go around and find what you want?" Jerry said to us. "Milk, cereal, whatever kids eat. If you see somethin' for dinner, go ahead and pick it up."

"Dinner?" Rache whispered to me. "We're supposed to going soon."

"Well, what do you have in that backpack of yours for dinner?" I asked.

She didn't have an answer for that. "Okay." Sigh. "We'll stay for dinner. But I don't think Jerry has a lot of money. Let's just pick out a couple things."

We walked the aisles over the yellowed tile floors, poking into dusty bins of candy or batteries that hadn't been changed out in years, probably. Finally, we decided on a big package of trail mix, some spaghetti noodles and a jar of sauce, and a six-pack of Cheerwine, and set it on the counter.

"Also, I'll take two dozen nightcrawlers," Jerry said.

Ed opened an ancient half refrigerator set on a crate behind the counter and pulled out two big paper cups full of dirt. "Alright, two dozen." He checked the price stickers on all our items and punched numbers on the cash register. "Okay, Jerry. Comes to twenty dollars and thirty-six cents."

Jerry already had his wallet out. He put his thumb and forefinger inside and pulled out a twenty, folded in half from top to bottom. He reached in his pocket and I saw his hand wriggling around in there. I knowed he was feeling for the right size coins. A quarter, a dime, a penny. He set 'em on the counter one at a time.

"No, sir." Rache looked puzzled. "Shouldn't be that much. It should come out to eighteen-something."

Ed shot her an irritated glance over his glasses but tore off the receipt from the register and examined it. "Hmm. I'm afraid you're wrong, young lady. Twenty thirty-six. Did you remember to include the tax?"

"I…I must have forgotten," Rache said. But I could tell with one look at her face she hadn't.

Now I had a suspicion about this guy. With his reading glasses and his white hair and his checkered shirt. Let me tell you, just 'cause someone looks like a friendly ole granddaddy don't mean he won't rip you off if he has half a chance. And choosing between him telling a lie and Rache getting a math problem wrong? There was no doubt who I believed. I got to thinking. Everything in the store we'd bought had a price tag on it, except one thing. "It was four dollars for those nightcrawlers, right Mister?"

Ed bit his lip. "Yes, four dollars."

"Oh, just four dollars?" Jerry said. "The nightcrawlers must be on sale this week."

"Umm—"

I cut Ed off. "Nope, sign outside says a dozen for

two dollars. Did you see it Rache?"

"Yes, that's what it says."

"Hmm." Jerry's expression didn't change but he tapped his walking stick on the floor a couple times. "What's that come to now, Ed?"

"Let's just call it eighteen even." Ed opened the register again and pulled out two one dollar bills.

Jerry took the bills and folded them in half from left to right before sliding them into his wallet. Meanwhile, Ed was staring me down like he was gonna set me on fire. But you know me. I stared right back 'til Jerry turned to go.

An old lady with over-sized sunglasses come in through the door at the same time we were leaving. "Oh Jerry! We don't usually see you except on Saturdays. And who's this you have with you?"

"Morning, Mizz Darlene. This here's my niece and nephew."

"Oh, how nice to meet you both." She held out her hand and Rache and me shook it. She peered at the cups Rache was holding. "What do you have there, young lady?"

"Nightcrawlers, ma'am. Uncle Jerry's taking us

fishing."

"Oh, how lovely. You know, the way you talk about them, Jerry, I expected they'd be older." She looked me up and down. "And you never told me the boy was adopted!"

"Oh, these are… my other sister's kids."

The lady put her finger to her lips and clicked her tongue. "Now let's see. Did I know you had two sisters?"

"I don't know if I've mentioned it before." Jerry pushed the door open a little too quickly. "C'mon, kids, we got to get back 'fore the fish stop biting. I'll be seeing you, Mizz Darlene."

"Oh! Bye then, Jerry."

Mizz Darlene shuffled towards the register and we went out. Here Boy slowly got up from where he'd been sleeping in the shade under the awning, stretching out his front legs. When I glanced back through the store window, Ed was watching us leave, staring at us hard over the tops of his glasses, like he was trying to kill me and Rache dead on the spot with the power of his eyeballs.

Chapter Eleven

Here Boy knowed it first, of course, keeping close to Jerry as we walked and whining softly while looking nervous at a spot up ahead on the gravel road.

"What's wrong with Here Boy?" Rache asked. "Doesn't he like going back home?"

"Oh, it's not that." Jerry sighed. "Why don't you kids take him and race back to the house? See who wins."

But Jerry's plan to spare us was too late. Here Boy let out a yelp like a yellow jacket stung his ass and a second later I felt something graze my forehead. I put my hand to the spot and when I drew it back bright red blood stained my fingers.

"Hey!" Rache yelled in surprise beside me.

At that point my mind sort of hazed and concentrated at the same time, 'cause I realized what it was, and it pissed me off. Somebody was throwing rocks at us.

I charged the spot, a place with a big pine tree where the road curved. They was laughing behind the tree, in book talk you'd say *snickering*, and I didn't care how big they was 'cause the blood was running in my eye, which made my feet run on the ground. I could hear Rache and Jerry yelling behind me but even they couldn't stop me now.

There was four altogether behind the tree trunk, and they was bigger than me but not too much, I'd say seventh graders. I jumped at the first closest one, some kid with braces and a pizza face, his eyes widening in surprise as I sailed through the air, fists already balling.

"Get off me, doofus," he said through a mouth full of pine straw after my flying leap knocked him to the ground, and I got in a couple licks but the others pulled me off before I really had the chance to bash him.

"Hey, the drunk old blindey got friends!" somebody

hissed in my ear, and I aimed an elbow in the direction of the voice but whoever was there grabbed my arm and twisted it so hard behind my back it arched my chest out.

Braces was back on his feet, advancing towards me with a metal-mouth grin. "That true? You friends with that greasy plastered hippie?" Giggles and snorts behind me.

"Let me go, you asshole!" I coiled and yanked but couldn't free myself from the unseen grip.

"You bleedin' above your eye, kid," Braces said. "Let's give you a nose job to match." He pulled his arm back and made a fist. And kept standing there without moving as something chunked against his temple.

A pretty biggish round river stone rolled to my feet. Braces swayed and I thought he was gonna fall out right there, but he caught ahold of himself and looked up stupidly, his arms dropping to his sides and his eyes glazing.

"What the hell?" came the voice behind me and the grip on my arm let go.

I turned to see but I didn't really need to. It wasn't no surprise. There stood Rache and she had another river stone in her left hand. "Who else wants one?"

The seventh graders hesitated. They were bigger but she could obviously aim. One of 'em muttered, "C'mon, y'all, this is bullshit," and they trudged off. Except Braces, still standing there with his mouth hanging open.

"Go on, you too," Rache said, and she took a step toward him. He shivered, a whole body shake, and it seemed to wake him up from his daze. He nodded slightly at Rache, like he was being introduced to her for the first time, and followed the others into the trees.

"You kids okay?" Jerry asked. I hadn't even thought about what he was doing this whole time.

I shook my arm out where the kid had jammed it behind my back. My shoulder was a little sore but it'd be fine. And when I wiped my t-shirt below my cut the blood was only a trickle. "I'm good," I said.

"No, you're not," Rache replied. "When we get back, we're getting the iodine out of the first aid kit in the backpack."

Great. She really hadn't forgotten to pack anything, even that evil stinging liquid Mama was always dabbing on with a cotton ball when I scraped my knees, as if they wouldn't heal fine without it.

* * *

Jerry's fishing spot was just up a bit from where our canoe was parked. It was a little grassy ledge on the edge of the river with a fallen log to lean against. Watching him, I think the secret to being blind is having a good memory for where you put things. When he needed a worm, he'd reach right over without fumbling at all to where he'd set one of those paper cups. He'd stick his fingers in the moist black dirt and pull out a fat wiggling nightcrawler, and with his other hand put his hook right through it. He only had one fishing pole but we passed it around so everybody got a chance.

"Do you eat the fish you catch?" Rache asked.

"Of course I do." Jerry was holding the pole and bobbed it up and down a bit. "But if the fish ain't bitin' I have to eat pork 'n' beans for dinner."

"I'm glad we bought that spaghetti then," I said.

"Me too," Jerry said.

It was pretty drowsy sitting there with the sun warm behind us but the dirt cool under our butts. Here Boy was asleep on top of the log and I might just have joined him except Rache had a new question. “How come you never call the cops on those boys who throw rocks at you?”

I raised my eyebrows at that. And she had the nerve to glare at me when I asked an awkward question! Still, I did have an interest in hearing what Jerry had to say.

“Oh, they ain’t there every day. It ain’t no trouble.”

“It is!” Rache protested. “Rocks hurt! And Here Boy can’t defend himself. You oughta get the cops to take them to jail.”

“They’ll grow out of it, eventually,” Jerry said. “And I don’t wanna get the cops involved. Bring that kind trouble down on those boys’ heads. Besides, cops come out here, maybe they start lookin’ round my place, and I don’t want that neither.”

“I’m with Jerry,” I said. “Better to handle it yourself than get the Law mixed up.”

Rache gave me a look meant I should shush. She wasn’t done yet with her questioning. “Has that man at the grocery store been ripping you off the whole time?"

"Hmm." Jerry switched the rod to his other hand. "Truth be told, I wish you hadn't brought up that matter with Ed."

"But it's not right he was overcharging you!" Rache said.

"No, it's not right." Jerry mused a bit. "But now he'll be ashamed every time I go into the store. We'll never be on friendly terms again."

"He's not really your friend if he's stealing your money."

"Maybe. I've been going to Ed's store a long time, though."

Rache set her jaw. "If you don't point out when somebody breaks the rules, they just keep right on doing it."

Jerry smiled and blinked a couple times over those white eyes. "I admire your spirit, Rache. You got a thirst for justice."

"Don't you have a thirst for justice?" Rache asked.

"The way I see it, sometimes it's better to ignore the little things a person does wrong and save your energy for the big things."

"The way I see it, a dollar every time you go in the store adds up to a big thing."

"Ha!" Jerry was really laughing now, bent over, his shaking jiggling the line into the water. "Well now, I hope you're paying attention, J.T. Never get in an argument with this lady. She'll talk you into doing the right thing, whether you want to or not."

"Don't I know it," I said. I waited to hear what Rache would bring up next, but either she was satisfied for the moment, or she was vexed 'cause Jerry had laughed at her. In any case, it got pretty quiet.

I rolled over on my stomach and leaned over the edge at a place where the bank kind of indented a little bit and the water was calm. On the surface there was about a dozen water skeeters flitting around, or as some people call 'em, Jesus bugs.

I guess I never really paid attention that close to 'em before. I just assumed they skated right across the water like they was floating. But now I saw, if you look real close, their feet actually make little dimples in the water, and if they move fast, they even make a tiny little splash. Maybe it seems like they ain't disturbing nothing, and most of the time they ain't, but still, every time they move it makes that tiny little impact. Nobody would ever expect that little impact to make any difference, but sometimes it must. I bet whole ships been sunk just 'cause a Jesus bug kicked its leg at exactly the right time, and the sailors on that ship never even knowed why they was swamped.

* * *

We never did catch no fish that afternoon. Jerry was too nice to say it, but it was 'cause of me and Rache's jawing the whole time, scaring 'em all off. It was a peaceful evening, both of us fascinated again just to watch Jerry find the pots and open the spaghetti sauce up and light the gas stove without seeing. Of course, he had no problem finding the beer, either. There was three empty cans on the table by the time we went to bed, and I suspect he mighta been holding back for our sake.

Brushing our teeth before bed was a conundrum. "Just skip it," I whispered to Rache, so Jerry wouldn't hear. "Or you wanna use that yellow water?"

Rache's face took on a disgusted expression.

"We could always use Cheerwine," I suggested.

Her face got even worse, but brightened. "I got an idea." She called out to the bedroom. "Jerry, may I use the stove?"

"You go right ahead," came his voice floating back.

She filled a big pot with water almost to the top and lit the stove. "Now all we got to do is wait for it to boil. Kill whatever's in there."

"Are you crazy?" I said. "We don't need that much water to brush our teeth."

"We can use the rest to fill up our canteen."

I got to admit, Rache is always thinking about the future. It took a damn long time for that water to boil, but I suppose we was watching it practically the whole time, and afterwards we had to wait for it to cool as well. Water was still yellow, but we brushed with it anyway.

Afterwards we laid our sleeping bags on the carpet in the living room, next to Jerry's recliner, and Here Boy laid right down between us. I suppose he figgered we needed him there more'n Jerry did.

"G'night, kids," Jerry said. He went to bed without

flipping off the kitchen light, which was shining right through the doorway and into our faces, and Rache and I looked at each other and laughed. Of course he wouldn't realize he needed to. So I got up and flipped it off. I think Rache was snoring before I made my way back.

* * *

I knowed something was wrong when Here Boy growled low and long and I felt his whole body tense. I opened my eyes. Jerry didn't have any curtains on his window so I could see stars and moonlight outside. I didn't know how long we'd been asleep but it was definitely the middle of the night. Here Boy let out a sharp bark.

Jerry was in the room in a jiffy, kneeling beside us and shaking us.

"Y'all got to get up," he said. "There's somebody a-comin'."

Chapter Twelve

I strained my ears but I couldn't hear nothing. But both Here Boy and Jerry had heard it. "How do you know?"

"Can't you hear it? The car wheels on the gravel road?"

Now that he'd pointed it out, I could hear it, and it was getting louder. I put my hand to the waistband of my jeans to check for the leather bag. It was still there. I'd been wearing it so long I hardly felt it anymore.

Rache was already out of her sleeping bag and pulling on her shoes and I did the same. I'd been pretty irritated before bed when she'd insisted on repacking the backpack all nice and neat but now I couldn't be more grateful.

"But couldn't it be somebody made a mistake?" I asked as I tied my laces. "Turned down the wrong way? Or maybe a friend of yours coming to visit?"

"Nobody but my sister come visit me for eight years. Those cars ain't no mistake."

Rache had her pack on and I grabbed the loose sleeping bags, still warm from our bodies. No time to roll those up nice and neat. Jerry held the back door open for us.

"I don't know what y'all are runnin' from, but you be careful out there. Can you see enough to make it to the river?"

"We can see in the moonlight." Rache gave Jerry a hug. "Thank you for everything."

"Oh, honey. Havin' you two here was the most excitement I had in years."

"What will you say to them?" I asked him, stopping on my way out the door.

"I'll say two kids stopped by so I fed 'em and they went on their way." He clapped me on the shoulder. "'Taint a lie, is it? Now get movin'."

Outside, it was light enough to pick our way through the woods. A pair of cars bounced down the gravel path, their headlights cutting jerky through the trees. Couldn't see the make of the cars, but I had no doubt who they were. We were about out of sight by the time they pulled up to Jerry's house. There was our canoe, right we'd left it yesterday morning at the place where the riverbank crinkled up.

"We might get wet pushing it in the water," I said.

"No help for it." Rache lowered her backpack in. "Toss in the sleeping bags. And let's put in our socks and shoes, too."

It turned out to be easier getting it back down on the river than it had been going up, but we still had muddy feet and was wet up to our knees before we got underway. I had knots in my gut in case we heard a gunshot, but it never came. So I guess Here Boy made it despite those dog-killers coming to his house.

It was pretty dark out but there was enough moonlight to tell where we was. We let the current do the work and dipped in a paddle occasionally to keep in the middle of the river, pulling it back out with a gurgle and setting it softly on the bottom. Otherwise, we glided along with only the sound of the insects singing. My feet was dry by now and I realized we did it again, we got away, and the knots in my gut slowly unwound. Neither of us was sleepy but it didn't feel like a time to talk either.

As I sat there I got to thinking this was the only thing real: me, Rache, the trees, the canoe, the river, the insects. This was the whole world, and anything else I remembered was fading in my brain. The fifth grade, the other kids at school, Daddy in prison up in Neuse, they was only like a dream after you wake up, and not an especially good one. Maybe this didn't have to end, it could always be this quiet and dark and calm, and me and Rache could be together forever, just floating.

But then I started thinking about the other things—the good things. My house, my room, Mama, my little brother Robby. How he used to come in my room and play with my army men when I was at school, and how angry I'd get coming home and finding 'em all messed up. I hoped he was playing with 'em all he wanted now I was gone.

After a while the sky started to turn a little gray, and purple and orange crept up on the undersides of the clouds, and it got bright enough I could see leaves on trees and things, and not just the shapes in the dark. That's when my stomach started tugging at me a little bit.

"Should we stop and make a fire soon?" I asked.

"What for?"

"To cook breakfast. Though I don't know if I can take going back to powdered eggs."

"We don't have to. We have the trail mix Jerry bought us."

"Oh, thank the Lord," I said. "I can't believe you remembered to pack that."

"Of course I did." She unstrapped the top of the backpack and pulled out the bag. She took a big handful and passed it to me. Nuts, almonds, raisins, M&Ms.

I washed down my handful with a drink from the canteen. "I think I'm getting more mature," I said.

"Why do you say that?"

"Before I woulda fished out all the M&Ms first, but today it seems right to eat the trail mix just how it is."

Rache laughed. "You think that's what makes you mature?"

"Well, not the only thing. Maybe it's a sign of it,

though."

"Could be."

I took another handful. "I been thinking. Maybe we should just give them pictures back if the sheriff wants 'em so much."

Rache's expression darkened. "I thought you said you hated those dog killers."

"I do! But if we gave 'em back, we could go home again. What do we want with those old pictures, anyway?"

"I swear to God, Jacob Thomas Honeycutt, if you're going soft on me I will push you out of this boat right now. I'm never going home again, so you get that out of your damn head."

I was pretty embarrassed by now, but I'd brought the subject up and Rache was already angry so I might as well see it through. "I don't even understand what we're supposed to do with the pictures. Who wants to see that?"

Rache clicked her tongue. "Nobody *wants* to see them. But when we show them to my friend in Wilmington, she'll be able to put those people in jail."

"I don't get it."

She started talking like a teacher explaining fractions to the slow kid in class. "Listen, J.T. My friend's a journalist. She works for the newspaper. The pictures show the grown-ups doing what they shouldn't. They're the proof. Laban, Sheriff Tate, all those lying bastards, caught breaking the law. When Laban goes to jail, that's when I'll be ready to go home. When it's just Mama and me again."

It's true the picture with Laban had showed him doing…*things...* with somebody who wasn't Aunt Marnie. I wasn't sure he'd go to jail over it though. But then a thought occurred to me. "Judge Satterfield too?"

"If he was in those pictures."

He had been. I could never forget his face. Not since that day in the courtroom, sitting on them hard pews next to Mama and with all the boring lawyer talk, and Judge Satterfield sitting in his big chair at the front and reading the sentence with the stoniest face you can imagine. A long face, drooping skin under the eyes, hardly no expression. Nobody else in the courtroom said a word when he spoke, only the buzzing of the fluorescent lights overhead, and his deep droning voice. Six years, he read out, like it was nothing, and Mama started to cry right next to me. Six years with no Daddy in our house. I wonder if the judge ever thought about me and Mama and Robby when he was pondering on his decision. If he ever thought on how empty our house would be, and how hard Mama'd have to work with Daddy gone.

And there he was in that photograph in the bag in my waistband, leaned over a table with a straw up his nose. I knowed it was drugs. Could he really go to jail for that? I would love to see that. But I wasn't real sure I believed it. I looked at Rache out the corner of my eye. "How well do you know this lady in Wilmington?"

"She'll remember me. You don't have to worry."

"Do you even know where she lives?"

"Duchess Street. I remember when she said it because it sounded so pretty."

"But do you—"

"Damn it, J.T.! Knock it off! I told you not to worry about it."

Rache's words shut my mouth, but they didn't calm my mind. Not this time. I highly doubted it was all going to work out like she thought. In my experience, when something sounds too good to be true, it means you're about to get taken.

Now that it was brighter I could see we was in a place where the river kept splitting. Floating along we'd use our paddle to steer into one stream or another, but just a little ways down it'd divide again 'til there must've been twenty different courses, all running next to each other, with long little strips of dry land between 'em. Sometimes the streams would join back together, but mostly they separated, the river widening so you couldn't even tell where the real shore began, and increasingly it wasn't even strips of land keeping the streams apart, but just trees growing straight up out of the black water.

"Which way should we take?" I asked once or twice.

"Doesn't matter," Rache said.

It was strange I hadn't been sleepy at all in the night but now the sun was up I kept drifting off. I don't know how long I'd been out at one point but I snapped wide awake when Rache started shouting.

"Stop the canoe! Right there!"

"What is it?" I blinked the blur out of my eyes.

"Look at that! The live oak!" She pointed at an oncoming island in the middle of the stream, almost a hill, with a giant old tree growing up in the middle and spreading its branches out over the water. I wouldn't be surprised if that tree was a thousand years old.

"It's a big tree," I agreed.

"Don't you see it? Steer over there."

"What?"

"Hanging down, the tire swing!"

I squinted and sure enough, a tire swing was hanging from one of the low branches right at the edge of the water. We grounded the canoe on the sandy bank and stripped down to our underwear in no time flat.

The swing was perfect. The rope hung down with enough length so you could swing way out over the water and jump off in a pool deep enough that you didn't touch the bottom. Or you could swing right back up on shore where a big fallen log gave you a place to stand on. When Rache and I both climbed on at the same time the swing would spin as we swung out, and we'd push each other trying to make the other fall and splash. I knowed we was laughing and screaming loud but there weren't nobody around to aggravate with our noise. I never did figger who put that swing there in the middle of nowhere but they couldn't have picked a better spot.

While we was playing the sun disappeared and the clouds kept getting lower and lower in the sky, swirling around overhead like the dirty water down a bathtub drain. I didn't pay it too much mind but it did keep creeping up on the edge of my brain, but somehow not quite noticing until I looked up at one point and realized the clouds were so low I couldn't see the top of the tree.

"You know what? I think I'm going to climb the tree," I said to Rache. "You wanna come with me?"

"Nah, I'm going to relax a little," she said. "You go on."

We put our dry clothes back on and I started climbing. The bark was rough but it was still easy to climb 'cause the gnarled old branches was so broad you could crawl right along one until another branch crossed, and then climb up on that one, and so on, all the way up. I must've been twenty feet up and I was about to yell at Rache to come join me but I seen she was curled up in a mossy patch on a rock, snoring away.

I kept climbing, and all those thoughts from earlier came back to trouble me. About the fifth grade and about old Joe with his guts blown out, about the slobbering dogs dying in the yard, and about Mama and Robby and Granny, and Daddy up in prison, and the judge and the sheriff, and about Laban marrying Aunt Marnie after appearing in those pictures with his limbs tangled up with another man. And about the old man all alone in the house where I broke the window, and Jerry, the nicest person I ever met, and how the folks in that town didn't treat him right. It all seemed so unfair, everything, the whole damn world, the old people lonely and the good people treated mean and the bad people doing what they feel and laughing over it later. My chest got tight and my breathing got hard and my eyes kind of blurry the more I thought. My brain swirled like those gray clouds, so close I could nearly touch 'em. But I kept climbing, one branch to the next, hardly paying attention to what I was doing.

I reached a point where I couldn't go no further.

The tree kept going, but I ain't no squirrel. I knowed better'n to try my weight on some twig, 'cause by now it was a long, long way down. Rache and the canoe were little squiggles below. How high was I? Fifty feet? A hundred? I could see way far out, the river stretching on to the front and the back for miles, and to the left and right trees to the horizon without a break. And I looked up, the treetop lost in those weird, misty clouds, strips of mist winding and wrapping around each other like they was living things. There was a little wind, but it wasn't cold, it was refreshing, and my whole body felt light and clean, and all those worries I'd had didn't seem important this high up. My head was clear, and now I had a new thought.

J.T., you're gonna do it. You really are. You gotta trust things'll work out how they're meant to. You and Rache are gonna get those pictures to Wilmington and after that the truth will come out. It ain't gonna be easy, but it's gonna happen if you don't give up.

I don't know how long I stared up, but at one point it seemed like the clouds thinned out a bit, and there was a little patch of blue, and up in that patch I almost imagined I could see people flying, just floating around in the air. And the next thing I remember, somehow the sun was coming up and I was on the soft mossy ground next to Rache, her hand resting on my chest, as if I'd been asleep the whole time. But I hadn't been. I was sure of that.

PART THREE

Chapter Thirteen

We'd been asleep since yesterday afternoon. Guess we'd been tired after leaving Jerry's in the middle of the night. Rache was up quick and going through her backpack again and again. I figgered she was getting it neat and perfect how she likes before we left but she kept clicking her tongue, which means she's irritated.

"How much money do you have?" she asked.

"Not much. I spent most of it on Marlboros for Granny." I rolled over onto my back. The moss was surprisingly comfortable, thick as a rug. "Why?"

"I got some bad news, J.T."

"What's that?"

"We're out of powdered eggs."

"Still waiting for the bad news."

She looked at me serious. "Well, we finished the trail mix too. And the cocoa. There's nothing for breakfast."

"We'll have to park the canoe somewhere and find a store or something," I said. "Wait. Were you asking me about the money 'cause you don't have any?"

"No," Rache said. "I brought my whole savings."

"How much?"

"Twenty-seven dollars."

"Twenty-seven dollars! Why're you asking me about money then? That's enough for like ten meals at McDonald's!"

"No way." Rache shook her head. "We've got to make it last. We need to shop at a grocery store so the money'll go further."

We pushed off into the river and tried to figger out a good place to stop and look for civilization. It ain't like there's billboards on the river—*gas and lodging, 10 miles ahead.* We did stop a couple times, actually, and I walked a little ways to see if there was anything there, but it was nothing but piney woods. It got pretty late with no luck, I don't know what time exactly, but the sun was way past noon and the day was getting to that lazy part of the afternoon and we still hadn't had a bite, and we was hungry in an awful way.

How long had it been since we'd eaten, anyway? Trail mix yesterday morning. The last real meal had been at Jerry's the night before that. Now when you wake up and you ain't eaten, that's not so bad, but as the sun rises through the morning your stomach gets hard empty. It starts to ache at the bottom, and then the ache creeps up the sides. The ache doesn't go away, either, but you do stop thinking about it, 'cause pretty soon all you can imagine is how nice it'd be to have a big plate of fried chicken in front of you, or juicy sausages, or mashed potatoes dripping with butter. And some time after that, you stop thinking altogether. You don't talk, you don't notice things. You just kind of exist. You stare around all dopey and without paying attention, which is how we nearly floated past exactly what we were looking for. Of course, if we'd knowed then what we learned later, we might've decided to keep going.

"Stop the canoe!" Rache said. "J.T.! Get your paddle out! This is it!"

"What?" I looked up confused. "What is it?" She pointed at something above the bank and sure enough, through the tree branches I could make out a white steeple in the distance. "A church? Do you think there's a grocery store nearby?"

"Who cares? It doesn't matter. They have to feed the hungry at a church. It's part of their rules."

"But what if they don't got any food there?"

As usual, she ignored questions she thought were stupid. "Get the other paddle out and help me." She was already steering us over.

We left the backpack in the canoe and walked up the back way to cross the church parking lot. Everything about it was crisp, somehow. The parking lot pavement was black like it was fresh-poured, with bright white lines for the parking spaces. The church was pretty big and could've been built last week it was so white, with covered walkways and buildings all full of shining windows. The big signboard out by the street said it was the New Life Salvation Bible Church, with Sunday services at 8, 9:30, 11, and a Saturday night casual service at 7.

We walked right in through the huge wooden

double doors at the front. Inside was all wood floors and gray-cushion folding chairs and beige-painted walls and powerful air-conditioning that kind of gave me a chill after being outside all that time. An office to the right had windows facing the hallway with blinds in 'em. I don't know why a room inside a building needs windows, but there it was. Anyway, the lights was on so we walked right up. A man in shorts and a t-shirt sat staring at a computer. He was pretty young, I think.

"Are you the preacher?" I asked.

He jumped a little and stared at us a moment before standing and smiling. "No, I'm the youth pastor here. Call me Brian. Are you two here with your parents?"

"No," Rache said. "We're just visiting. Could we speak with whoever is in charge?"

Brian nodded. "That'd be Pastor Jim. Wait here a minute. I'll be right back."

He headed off down some hallway. Rache sat in a folding chair and I read some of the Bible verses they had in gold frames on the walls. It was all faith and hope and love and whatnot. I don't got too much

Bible-learning but I heard some of the stories. These wasn't stories, though, only sentences cut out that sound nice, but don't really mean much.

Brian came back with Pastor Jim, whose belly filled out his khaki pants and blue shirt with buttons like he didn't miss too many meals. He had curly brown hair and glasses and he bent down with his hands on his knees to talk to us at eye level.

"I'm Pastor Jim. What can I do for you two?"

"We were… we were wondering if you had something here we could eat," Rache said. I was embarrassed at her words, especially 'cause I realized how we must look. We hadn't changed clothes since we'd left Wyattville, and I couldn't even think how many days that'd been. Hadn't bathed, either. At Rache's insistence we'd at least brushed our teeth a few times. But I knowed we looked dirty. On the river or with Jerry that'd been fine. But now, in this white clean church, with Pastor Jim looking at us with his brown eyes all sad and sorry-feeling for us, I was embarrassed. No, that ain't the right word. I was *ashamed.*

Pastor Jim rose. "Brian, I think we have some

birthday cake from the staff meeting left in the kitchen refrigerator. And bring back a couple bottled waters too, would you?" Brian walked off and Pastor Jim studied us. "Do your parents live nearby?"

Rache hesitated. "No, sir."

Clearly we had to explain ourselves, at least a little, but it was hard to tell how much. Better if we gave enough of a hint so Pastor Jim wouldn't get too curious right away, but without really explaining anything. Kind of like those Bible verses on the walls. "We had to leave," I said. "Things wasn't too good at home."

"Not since my step-father moved in," Rache said.

"Oh, you poor children." Pastor Jim shook his head at the hardness of it all. "And isn't the Lord good to lead you right to us."

He stepped forward and I thought he was going to hug us, which I ain't too fond of, but I coulda bore it. But what he actually did was reach out and run his fingers through my hair, which surprised me so much I didn't even react at all. Or maybe I was so eager to have that birthday cake I didn't want to spoil anything. Damn fool mistake on my part.

"Oh, she's going to love you two," he said in a low tone. I didn't know what to say to that, and Rache must not have either. It wasn't even clear he was talking to *us* at all. "She is going to love you two so much."

Chapter Fourteen

After the birthday cake, which tasted like Jesus himself came down to bake the chocolate and spread the vanilla icing on top, and with Pastor Jim and Brian sitting there in the gleaming kitchen watching us stuff our faces, Pastor Jim asked us if we wanted to join him at his home for dinner. Now two slices of cake had barely took the edge off the hunger, so there was hardly a decision to make. We didn't even have to check with each other, we both said "Yes" at the same time.

In the parking lot he used a remote control to beep open a black BMW 730i. My eyes almost popped out my head 'cause I never been in a car like that before.

"Is this your car?" I asked.

He chuckled. "Of course. Climb on in and we'll get going."

It was as fancy on the inside as you'd imagine, all leather and wood, and Pastor Jim drove through a lot of twisty roads while me and Rache sank back in those soft felty seats and watched the trees go by through the tinted windows. I waited on the drive for all the questions. *Where are you from? Who are your parents? Why did you run away? How did you get here?* But they never came. All the time we was there, Pastor Jim and Mizz Belinda never asked a single thing about our past. But I'm getting ahead of myself.

After driving so many roads there wasn't no way to remember, we came to this big gate with iron bars where he rolled down his window and put in a code on a keypad. The gate slowly swung open by itself and we drove through and there was nothing but giant houses, all built practically next to each other with hardly no grass between 'em, only short little trees spaced out front just so. Laban would've loved this place.

Pastor Jim's house was at the back of the neighborhood, and it was the biggest house of all. I mean, I can't even describe what it looked like overall 'cause it was too much to look at all at once, just a huge pile of tan bricks, with different wings jutting out and about a million circular windows and roofs sloping down. It was a little different than the other houses too, 'cause it did have a yard, a big one sloping up to the woods in back, with a buncha buildings behind. Pastor Jim used an automatic opener to open the widest garage door I ever seen and pulled in between a red BMW 318 and a brown Chevy conversion van.

We followed him in the house, and this'll sound silly 'cause the house wasn't *that* big, probably I was confused from not eating enough, but I don't know if I coulda found my way back out again. Down a hallway and up some stairs and across a walkway over a living room and still another hallway and yet another small set of stairs and then we came to a bathroom with two sinks, one on either side, and in the middle a sit-in tub with a tiled step up to it.

Rache let out an "mmm" when she saw the bathroom and I thought she might start purring right there.

"I'll be back with a towel in a minute," Pastor Jim said. "You go ahead and get started. I'll leave the bath towel right inside the door."

He led me to my own bathroom, not quite as fancy, but still with enough white tiles and silver faucets for my whole house back in Wyattville. I also had to use a shower instead of a giant bathtub, but that didn't bother me either. I hadn't missed taking baths, but I had to admit, now that I stepped into the hot water it was relaxing. I even used shampoo in my hair which I never do at home, which drives Mama crazy.

When I got out not only was there a big fluffy pink towel, but a clean t-shirt too, with New Life Bible Salvation Church printed across the front of it. Same jeans and underpants as before, but I guess Pastor Jim don't got extras of those just laying around.

I dressed and wandered out into the hallway and made my way back to Rache's bathroom. I leaned my head in. "How long you gonna take?"

"Go away, J.T.! I'll be out when I'm out."

I figgered she would take her time in there, females always do, and I didn't hear no sign Pastor Jim was nearby, so I thought I'd take a little walk around. I poked my head in a couple bedrooms but they were pretty normal. There was one locked room at the top of its own private half-staircase which was interesting. I considered picking the lock but I didn't want to bother so I made my way down to the kitchen, big and fancy as you might expect, with eight burners on the stove on an island and two ovens and two refrigerators. Why two? I guess Pastor Jim liked to pack it away. At the back there was a big set of sliding glass doors leading out onto a courtyard. I was fixing to check one of the fridges for a bite but I heard a basketball bouncing from the courtyard and my curiosity got the better of my hunger.

The courtyard was covered with paving stones and there was buildings on each side--the house behind me, some wooden barns to the left and right, and the sound of the basketball was coming from an open metal door in the building in front, which must have been some kind of gym. I could hear shoes squeaking now, too, and the sounds of kids yelling.

There was three picnic tables in the middle of the courtyard, some big wooden pots with pink flowers and things in 'em, and a couple big wicker hampers at the side. I had the idea there might be some kinda food in one of those hampers and I'd be able to get a glimpse inside the door of the gym too, so it'd be killing two birds with one stone. I was about to lift the top when a voice almost made my jump out my skin.

"Who are you?" It was a teen-ager leaning against the doorframe of the gym with a basketball under one arm and staring me down.

I shoulda stared right back but I was so surprised all I did was say, "J.T." The teen-ager gave a slight nod. I guessed from his height he was probably about thirteen, with curly hair cut close to his head and light brown skin. He wore a gray t-shirt with the same church logo as mine, and had a long raised scar down his jawline. He didn't say nothing else, just leaned there. Of course if I talked first he would win, but my growling stomach threw me off my game and I gave in after a minute. "What's your name?"

"You suppose be here?" He spoke with a Spanish accent.

"I think so," I said. "Pastor Jim brought us."

"I mean, you suppose be here sneaking in those baskets?"

By now some other kids had gathered behind him and were trying to see out but he didn't bother removing himself from the doorframe. "Who is it?" "Is there someone new?"

"Don' worry about it." He pushed 'em back in and pulled the door closed behind him.

Just then, the sliding glass door opened behind me. "There you are! You shouldn't have wandered off!" said Pastor Jim's chiding voice, but I kept looking at that gym door.

* * *

Rache and I sat on stools at a counter in the kitchen eating American cheese slices, which I normally hate, but right about then Pastor Jim coulda put dog food on a plate and we would've said how tasty it was. We could hear the front door open and Pastor Jim stood up from the desk where he sat working at a computer. "Honey, come on to the kitchen. I have a surprise for you!" He signaled with his hand for us to stand up and when we did, he put his hands on our shoulders to position us side by side. "Stand up straight," he whispered. "She doesn't like slouching."

Mizz Belinda, 'cause we found out soon that was

her name, came in the room like a hot pink swish. That was the sound she made when she moved, and that was what she looked like. Everything about her was hot pink—high-heeled leather boots, skirt, blouse, jacket, lipstick, almost her curly hair, too, though that was really more strawberry. She even talked hot pink, if that makes any sense. "This better be good, Jim, because I have had a fucking day today and you would not believe—" She stopped when she saw us. Her eyes widened like a little kid's at Christmastime and her mouth opened just slightly, turning up at the corners. "Where did you get these?" She stretched out the "where" 'til it was practically two words.

"They showed up at the church hungry and I brought them home. Is the Lord good?"

She turned and gazed at Jim for the first time since she'd entered the room. "Oh, the Lord is good, honey."

Pastor Jim's voice turned deeper and hoarser and he stepped in front of Mizz Belinda. "And Daddy? Is Daddy good?"

"Daddy is very good." She ran a hot pink nail-polished finger down his cheek and to his chest. "But he'll get his reward later." She playfully pushed him away and turned back to us, bending over to be on our level and inspecting us up and down, Rache first and then me. Rache and I exchanged looks.

"Their names are Rache and J.T.," Pastor Jim said.

She ignored him completely. I didn't like this whole procedure, like we was horses or dogs or something. If she'd reached out to pinch my cheek I was fixing to belt her one, even if she was a girl. But fortunately for her, she asked the right question. "He said you were hungry. What did Pastor Jim feed y'all?"

"Birthday cake," Rache said.

"And…."

"And American cheese," I added.

She stood back up and put her hands on her hips. "Jim, I don't know what you're thinking. These kids are starving. Look how skinny they are! They have got to eat."

"I thought I'd wait until we were all ready to eat together, sweetie." His voice pleaded a little bit, like he was afraid she'd get angry.

Mizz Belinda clapped her hands three times. "Dinner, right now."

"Really? It's only half past five and I thought—"

But she was already out in the courtyard where she picked up a brass handbell and rang it fast. The gym door banged open and all the kids came outside and lined up, the Spanish-accent kid I met earlier at the head, I suppose 'cause he was the oldest, with everybody shorter lining up next to him. There were four boys and four girls, and the main thing I noticed was they looked like one of those ads for McDonald's where they don't want to leave out nobody—black, white, Chinese, Mexican, whatever. Pastor Jim and Mizz Belinda had one of each.

Mizz Belinda addressed the Spanish kid. "Angel, we're eating early tonight. Get everything set up and go get everyone cleaned up. And set two extra places." She turned and swished back into the house. Angel started pointing to other kids and giving orders. It turns out the wicker hampers held plates and cups and silverware and things, and they all got everything set up in a hurry before disappearing into the barns on either side.

Pastor Jim escorted me and Rache out in the courtyard and pointed us into the barns. "Go on in and get cleaned up." He pointed to the left—"That's the boy's side"—then to the right—"and the girl's side."

I never did get to see the inside of the girls' barn, but the boys' side reminded me of a navy ship or something. There was bunk beds at one end, a bunch of dressers and desks in the middle, and the bathroom at the other end. The floor was bare wood and there wasn't no pictures or nothing in the walls, just a big cross on the end near the bunk beds. Angel had each kid going in the bathroom, making sure they'd cleaned their faces and hands when they came back out. "You no use soap, go back in" to one, or "don't forget dry your hands" to another.

The handbell rang again and when we went back out Pastor Jim and Mizz Belinda was bringing out platters of hot dogs and hamburgers, big Tupperware bowls of cole slaw and potato salad, and pitchers of water and lemonade. I tried to sit at a table with Rache but felt a hand on my shoulder.

"That's the girls' table, son," Pastor Jim said. He nodded at another one. "The boys' table's over there."

So I sat with the boys at the other picnic table, the girls at theirs, and the adults at the one closest to the house. All the food was in front of us and of course I was ready to dig in but Pastor Jim stood at the front and said, "Grace, everybody." We all bowed our heads and he started in with "Dear Lord" and kept on going. I mean, I was ravenous, and I had that food right in front of me, the buns and dogs smelling all warm and juicy, and when Pastor Jim kept talking I opened my eyes and tilted my head up a little to see and I spied Rache at her table doing the same. Everyone else though, even the little ones, even Mizz Belinda, had their eyes closed. I thought that prayer would never end but finally Pastor Jim got to the "Amen" and we all repeated it.

After scarfing my first hot dog in about ten seconds I was still hungry and put another on my plate from the serving dish in the center of the table. But the ketchup was in front of Angel. "Hey Angel, could you pass the ketchup, please?" I was trying, right? How much more polite could I be?

"My name's not Ángel," he said. Somehow the name sounded Spanish in his mouth. Somehow his tone made it sound like I'd slapped him instead of asking nicely for something.

"That's what Mizz Belinda called you."

He regarded me coldly. "My name is Ramon."

One of the little boys spoke up here, a Chinese kid I'd heard someone call Hyun-Soo. "Angel his middle name, but only Mizz Belinda can call him that."

Angel/Ramon was pissing me off something mighty but I was still hungry and just wanted the ketchup so I could get on with eating. "Would you please pass the ketchup, *Ramon?*" I said. "Or did your name change again already?"

He passed it without comment. I wondered if things were going this dumb at Rache's table.

I ate about half a dozen hot dogs and plenty of sides, and cookies for dessert. I'll give Pastor Jim and Mizz Belinda one thing. They never skimped on the food. After dinner Ramon assigned kids various jobs—carrying dishes to the sink, or washing them, or drying, or wiping the tables off, or what have you, and we got it all clean faster than you'd think.

It was still light out and we all sat back down at the picnic tables, again boys at one table and girls at the other. I was getting antsy about that 'cause I wanted to talk to Rache and find out if the girls' barn was like the boys' and what she thought of everything and if we'd spend the night here or what, but that'd all have to wait. Anyway, since we were sitting back down it seemed like we might have ice cream or something but actually Pastor Jim got out a guitar and we sang a couple Bible songs, which wasn't too bad, even if Mizz Belinda looked goofy clapping daintily with her hands so as not to break her long, hot-pink fingernails.

At bedtime all the kids went into the barns and changed for bed. That's what all the dressers was for, of course. It wasn't like each dresser had your own clothes though, but that each one held a different kind of clothes. For instance, tonight, we went to the dresser that held pajamas, and everybody got out their pair. "You jus' find pajama that fit you close," Ramon told me. "If you no find one that fit good, we tell Pastor Jim tomorrow."

Since the other boys was taking showers, I headed out to the courtyard to try to meet Rache. I shoulda knowed Ramon would be up my ass like a stuck turd.

"Hey, where you goin'?" he said.

"I already took a shower."

"Yeah. But where you goin'?"

I was getting awfully hot about him by now, but

still didn't want no trouble here, especially since Pastor Jim had fed us and all. I swallowed down what I had the notion to say and kept it under control, though I did ball up my fists behind my back. "I'm gonna talk to my friend."

"The girls takin' showers. Leave 'em alone."

Fine. We obviously wasn't gonna get no peace with Sergeant Bringdown around anyway. I'd just wait 'til everybody was asleep and go out and meet Rache. I knowed she'd do the same and we'd figger things out then.

We all climbed in our bunks. I got a bottom bunk, with Hyun-Soo on top. The pajamas didn't feel tight enough to keep the leather pouch in the waistband, so I put it under my pillow.

Ramon had his own bunk bed to himself, where he slept on the bottom. His bed had a little reading lamp attached, which none of the others did. After everybody was ready, Pastor Jim showed up and gave a bedtime prayer, not too long this time, asking we all be blessed and sleep well and whatnot. After the amen he clicked the overhead lights off and pulled the door to the barn closed. There was a clicking sound from the door like it was being locked from outside. And that's when my stomach dropped out.

"Did he just lock us in?" I asked out loud. No one answered so I tried again. "Did Pastor Jim lock us in here?"

"No talking." Ramon's voice.

Damn. Why hadn't I figgered a way to talk to Rache earlier? Was she in the other barn in the same situation? She must be. "Hey, Hyun-Soo," I whispered. "Did Pastor Jim lock us in here?"

"Yes," came Hyun-Soo's whisper. "He open it in morning."

"I said, no talking," Ramon said again.

"Why?" I said. "Talking at night against the law here?"

The reading light snapped on from Ramon's bed and he came over to my bunk. He grabbed my pajama top with both hands and pulled me out. "Stand up."

"What the hell do you want?" I said, stumbling out of bed.

"You and your little girlfrien', you new here, so I tell you one time. Pastor Jim and Mizz Belinda is weird, but we eat good, we have clothes, we safe. You follow the rules, we good. If you fuck things up for us, I mess you up. You understan' me?"

I glared at him. I put a little extra on it 'cause he'd gotten the best of me earlier outside the gym when I'd been hungry.

He gripped my pajama shirt tighter and pulled my face close to his. The scar along his jawline was purple against his brown skin. "I said, you understan' me?"

"Yeah," I said.

He let me go. "And in the morning, you can tell your girlfrien' too." He went back to his bed and snapped off the light.

Chapter Fifteen

It wasn't 'til the next morning before breakfast I was able to talk to Rache again. Breakfast was a pretty similar procedure to the night before, with the kids setting the tables outside and everything, although Pastor Jim didn't really cook this time, just put out some toasted bread and peanut butter and big jugs of orange juice. Rache and I steered towards each other by one of the hampers.

"We gonna leave today or what?" I whispered to her.

"Yeah. But how are we gonna get back to the church?"

"Walk, I guess. Does it matter?"

"Yes, it does." Rache pulled out a Ziploc bag of

silverware from the hamper. "Do you remember your way back on all those winding roads? Plus it's like ten miles, at least. A lot more if we get lost."

Somebody cleared his throat behind us. I looked over my shoulder and there was Ramon. I ignored him. "Pastor Jim works at the church, right? It shouldn't be too hard to get a ride back there."

"Okay, then," Rache said. "We wait for our opportunity to go to the church. And as soon as we get there, we slip out and run for it."

Ramon butted himself between us. "You telling your girlfrien' what I told you to say?"

"Yeah, sure," I said to him. And one last thing to Rache: "Agreed."

But it didn't work out that morning. Pastor Jim went off to church by himself after breakfast, leaving us kids with Mizz Belinda. She wasn't real involved, actually I think she just woke up. Her pajamas was hot pink and her hair was all up in curlers, and without her make-up her eyes was kind of puffy. She drank coffee from a huge hot pink mug that read "World's Greatest Mom."

When everything was cleaned up she handed out

workbooks in the courtyard with a bored look. We was supposed to read in 'em and write the answers to questions. She told all the other kids to start in the place where they'd left off the day before and finish the next section or do a certain number of pages, but she didn't know about Rache and me.

"What grade are you two in?" she asked.

"We just finished the fifth grade," Rache said.

"Well, try these and see how far you get." She rifled through a big tote bag and handed us workbooks for the sixth grade, one about reading comprehension, one about math, and one about geography. She yawned and turned to Ramon. "I'm going back to bed. You handle things out here."

Ramon herded us all back to our barns. In the boys' barn, we sat at the desks, each with a little lamp on it. I opened all the drawers in mine, and it had the supplies you'd expect, pencils and notebook paper and pink erasers and whatnot. "Is this all we do?" I asked Ramon.

"All you need to worry about." I must not have picked up my pencil fast enough or something 'cause he pointed at my three workbooks. "So get to work."

It was pretty boring. We did the workbooks for two hours exactly, with a ten-minute break in the middle for the bathroom. During the break, I slipped out into the courtyard and tried all the sliding glass doors to the kitchen. Locked, naturally. Next I inspected the wooden slat fences connecting the house and the barns and the gym. No gates, and I guessed the fences at about eight feet tall, though I figgered in a pinch you could pull over a picnic table and climb over. Pastor Jim and Mizz Belinda sure wanted us locked in tight.

I felt somebody's eyes on me and turned to find Ramon in the barn doorway with his arms crossed. "Break time over."

"Just getting some fresh air, warden." I sauntered past him and back to the workbooks.

Now I ain't no great student, but the workbooks was pretty easy. A teacher would say they didn't *challenge* me enough, although I admit I did skip the math book altogether 'cause I just ain't doing math during summer break. If it was easy for me I have to imagine Rache must've got through about half the pages in each one. I did read some of the stories in the reading comprehension book and they wasn't too bad, but it wasn't long before I had my fill.

Those well-stocked desks turned out to have paper clips and rubber bands in 'em, and that's just what I needed to build a little slingshot. I cut up some notebook paper and folded it over to make little missiles to shoot. Hyun-Soo was at the desk a few feet over and I missed my first couple shots but then I got him straight in the ear. His head snapped up in surprise but when he saw what I'd made he grinned and went to work making one too and soon we had a little war going on.

"Do your work, stop messing 'round," Ramon called over.

His words didn't stop nothing, me and Hyun-Soo kept on firing our little missiles so Ramon stood up and moved me to his desk so he could sit between us. I tried to do some more workbook pages, I really did, but it wasn't gonna happen. I guess I was making a lot of noise and distracting everybody 'cause whenever I turned to look Ramon was glaring at me, and I glared right back. Finally the two hours was up and Ramon got everybody up, and poked his head in the girls' barn too, and we all went to the gym.

The gym was only big enough for half a basketball court. I mean, still pretty impressive they had it in their backyard, but it wasn't full-sized. Ramon divided the five boys into teams, me and Hyun-Soo and an African kid about six years old named Jumoke on one side, and himself with a Russian kid named Dmitry who hardly spoke any English. It was pretty lopsided when we started playing. I mean, Jumoke wasn't bad for a little kid, but he couldn't even throw the ball high enough to hit the net, so it was basically me and Hyun-Soo against Ramon and Dmitry. Hyun-Soo turned out to have some moves, but so did Dmitry so they canceled each other out, and Ramon was older and taller than everybody so he could block our shots. The score was about twenty to six against Hyun-Soo and me in no time.

The girls stayed off the court and jumped ropes or did clapping games. Rache was the oldest by quite a bit—I think the other four girls went from about four to not much older than Jumoke. It didn't surprise me a bit when after a few minutes she approached the boys.

"Which team am I on?" she asked Ramon.

He held up a hand. "No, no, no. You don' play with us. Girls play over there." He hooked a thumb at the sidelines.

"You don't have even teams," Rache said. "You need another player."

"We fine." Ramon rolled his eyes at the door. "You play wit' us, she no gonna like it."

But I knowed something about Rache that Ramon didn't, and I happened to be holding the ball. I passed it to her and she dribbled once and shot from where she stood, right outside the three-point line. It arced through the air and swished the net clean.

Ramon's eyebrows rose and he took a second to consider. "Okay. We give it a try."

"How 'bout this?" I said. "Me and Rache on one team, and we'll take Jumoke too, against the rest of you."

Ramon laughed—me and a girl and a little kid against them?—but he wasn't laughing long. My job was basically to feed Rache, so we'd pass the ball back and forth, toss it to Jumoke once in a while so he could be part of it, and as soon as Rache broke free of the defense she'd sink one, shot after shot. It was really embarrassing when she drove on Ramon and he couldn't stop her. And even after he and Hyun-Soo started double-teaming her it still didn't help, 'cause now only Dmitry was guarding me and, like I said, Dmitry wasn't bad, but I had a couple inches on him, so Rache'd pass *me* the ball and I'd go for it. My shots weren't as pretty as Rache's, tended to roll around the rim a few times or chunk off the backboard, but I made a few. I think the score was about thirty to twelve when our game was interrupted by the handbell ringing from the gym door.

We all turned. It was Mizz Belinda, now dressed and made-up for the day, hot pink everything but a completely different set of clothes than yesterday, and now the color of her face matched her outfit too. Her shriek echoed across the gym. "What the hell do you think you're doing?" I couldn't for the life of me figger what she was pissed about.

Nobody spoke. She stomped in with her high heels right up to Rache, who stood at the foul line with the ball under her arm. "I said, young lady, what do you think you're doing?"

"Playing basketball?" Rache said, no idea what was

going on here.

"No!" Mizz Belinda slapped her hard across the face, her eyes mean and her nostrils flared. Rache stood like a stone, she was so shocked. "That is not what young ladies do." She rang the bell. "Ladies! All of you, yes please. You too, Fatima. Time to go in the house." The young girls all jumped up and lined up at the door. Mizz Belinda pointed to Rache. "C'mon, in line. Time to go."

Rache didn't move at first, Mizz Belinda's handprint in red on her cheek. I could tell her eyes was wet. Not from pain, she wouldn't care about that, but from anger. I was pretty sure she was gonna refuse, maybe give Mizz Belinda a taste of what made her the cussingest girl in fifth grade, but to my surprise she finally dropped the ball and followed. She threw a hurt look back at us. Ramon shrugged. *I tried to tell you.*

* * *

We kept on shooting baskets and I wondered where Mizz Belinda had taken Rache and the other girls off to. Should I go look for her? But I didn't know what I would do when I found her. Maybe we should leave, just walk out the front door, take our chances with finding our way back to the river? But I had the feeling Mizz Belinda wasn't gonna let us go. Even if she couldn't physically stop us, she could call Ramon, she could call Pastor Jim, worst of all she could call the cops. Me and Rache had gotten in deep here without realizing it.

The boys had played what seemed liked twenty games of Horse when one of the girls, the cute little Chinese girl named Shao-ching, stuck her head in the door and said, "Come on inside! We got something to show you boys!"

Ramon sighed. "C'mon, we gotta see."

Mizz Belinda was waiting in a long living room with an arched ceiling where somebody'd pushed all the dazzling white furniture against one wall to make a kind of gallery down the middle. She perched on the edge of a loveseat in her hot pinkness with a big round wine glass in one hand and gestured with the other at the couches. "Have a seat boys, we'll get started in a minute." Ramon tried to sit away from her but she patted the cushion next to her on the loveseat. "Angel, baby, come sit by me."

Her eyes shone. Whatever was about to happen she was excited about. She called out, "Mei-tal, start the music!"

Of course the house had a built-in sound system and some kind of jazz started up with a lot of high-hat, a sound I recognized from our time with Jerry. Mizz Belinda clapped three times and the first girl came out. It was the little middle-Eastern girl, Nuzha, and she wore a sparkly silver dress. Her hair was done up and she had on make-up to match the outfit, not just silver sparkly lipstick but eyeliner and fingernail polish and everything.

"Walk just like I told you, honey," Mizz Belinda said, and Nuzha put one hand behind her head and sashayed down the gallery. Mizz Belinda clapped when she reached the end of the room and went out into the hallway. Ramon clapped too and when none of the rest of us joined in, Ramon gave us a look and we all started.

All the girls had their chance and the boys clapped politely after each one. Mizz Belinda rubbed Ramon's shoulders the whole time or traced her long fingernails across the back of his neck. Sometimes she'd lean over to whisper something to him and he'd laugh at her comment, but there was something that told me he wasn't enjoying it. He sat up a little too straight, was a little too quick to start clapping. For a moment I felt sorry for him.

Rache came out last and I couldn't help snickering when I saw her. She didn't have on make-up but she did have her hair up, and was wearing some kind of glittery red dress. Seeing Rache in a dress was too funny. I mean, I couldn't stop myself. But I stopped when I noticed that helpless look on her face, and I knowed why it was there. Here was a problem she couldn't dribble, punch, or cuss her way through. The only thing she could do was bear it. Her eyes though, they showed exactly what she was feeling: pure disgust.

* * *

Another day, another night. It went on the same every day. If I wanted I could explain to you more about how lunches went or the Bible lessons in the afternoon or dinnertime again with the singing afterwards. I could tell you about Mizz Belinda always having a wine glass in her hand or disappearing for hours and coming home with armfuls of department store shopping bags or Ramon always being on my case and my giving it back to him just as good. Don't matter though. Me and Rache was pissed and angry and bored out of our skulls.

I don't know, maybe all that time on the river ruined us. Once you get used to freedom, being able to do whatever you want, how can you live like Pastor Jim and Mizz Belinda wanted us to? I mean, I appreciate what they done for us. The food, the clothes, even the praying and Bible lessons was them trying to help us. But I could tell by looking at Rache, every move of hers tense like an animal in a cage, and that disgust in her eyes that started with the fashion parade and never went down. She was ready as hell to leave, and I was too. Just as soon as we got our chance.

Chapter Sixteen

Sunday morning was something different. Pastor Jim was out in the courtyard ringing that handbell way earlier than usual 'cause he had to leave early to preach, and Mizz Belinda came personally to each kid with the Sunday clothes she'd picked for us to wear. She even had new outfits for me and Rache, in our size and everything.

I didn't know what to think about my clothes, actually. I mean, khaki pants and a striped button-down shirt ain't exactly my style, and they was itchy to put on, besides. But it was the first time in my life I ever had new clothes, and I have to admit I was a little proud too, even if the pants was a little loose around my waist.

Rache, though. I mean, I knowed Rache all our lives, and she's always worn her Carolina athletic gear, except the couple days before when Mizz Belinda made her wear that glittery crap. But her dress today, it fit her. I don't mean it was the right size. I mean, it was dandelion yellow and clingy-stretchy and it flowed down her legs and had sleeves to her elbows and straps and everything. I don't know, I was acting stupid, like I'd never realized she had arms and legs before. She'd always been just Rache. But now, I couldn't stop looking at her at breakfast.

Fortunately for me, she didn't understand what my looks meant, and thought I'd been trying to get her attention. "Today's the day," she whispered to me as we cleaned up afterwards. "When we get to church, the second all the grown-ups aren't looking, we slip outside and run for it."

I nodded. I'd been thinking the same thing.

* * *

We all piled into the brown Chevy conversion van in the garage and Mizz Belinda backed out the driveway like the house was on fire. She took those twisty turns at a speed that made me wonder if the van might topple over.

The inside of the van was plush—carpets and deep seats and even a table with a magnetic top where you could play checkers in the back while the van was driving. Nobody did though. Ramon sat in the passenger seat up front and even with nine kids there was plenty of room left over in back. It was weird. Mama can't even drive me and my little brother Robby to the grocery store without us fighting in the backseat, but somehow with all those kids in the van the whole trip to church was perfectly quiet. Fine by me, though. I spent my time staring at the window, trying to memorize the roads. Sure me and Rache intended to run this morning, but if it didn't work out, we might need to know the way later.

When we pulled up to the church, she lined us up in the parking lot to fuss over us. "Stand up straight, Fatima. Dmitry, brush those crumbs off your shirt. Best behavior from everybody today. Especially you two," she said, staring right at me and Rache.

When we went in, I got why she cared so much all

of a sudden. At home, she might've barely paid attention to us, but here at church, Mizz Belinda was having the time of her life, showing off her two latest additions to everybody she could find. "When I laid eyes on these two precious children for the first time I just had to help them," she'd say to anybody who stopped to gab. "It's just how I am. We are so blessed the Lord delivered them into our lives." And then she'd shove us right at some fat ancient couple who'd probably known Robert E. Lee personal, and who'd coo over us without actually paying any attention. "Well, bless their hearts," Mrs. Got-Rocks or Old Lady Big-Ass or Old Man Pee-Smell would say.

"You should've seen how skinny they were when we found them," Mizz Belinda'd go on. "But they are blooming so much since they've had the chance to be in a real, loving family." As if our four days at her house doing workbook pages was making all the difference.

It was youth pastor Brian who almost made me and Rache flip, though. As we passed by his office with the windows on the inside he waggled his finger at us to come in.

"I hope you two realize how lucky you are," he said. "It's such a blessing for both of you." And he stood there smiling with his hands folded in front of him.

I figgered he was just talking about us staying with Pastor Jim or whatever and Rache must've too so we thanked him and turned to go out the door.

"You're welcome. I just wanted to be the first to congratulate you."

Now my suspicion got up a little and I stopped, twisting my head slightly. "What for?"

His face turned kind of pale. "Oh, haven't they told you yet?"

Me and Rache turned back around.

"They haven't told you yet." He popped himself on the head with his knuckles. "I shouldn't have said anything."

"Told us what?" Rache asked.

His voice turned whispery like he had a big secret. "I shouldn't say. I'm sure they wanted to tell you themselves. Jim and Belinda are going to adopt you!"

A half-smile stayed on his face, like he was waiting for a big happy reaction. But me and Rache didn't say nothing. I mean, no words would come out from the shock.

The half-smile faded. He stood and put his hands on our shoulders. "It's a lot to think about, isn't it? I know how you must feel. Pastor Jim told me all about your home and your stepdad and how terrible he used to treat you two."

There was a lot of questions I had to push down right then. *Why is Pastor Jim making up stories he don't know nothing about?* Also, *was he and Mizz Belinda planning on ever telling us about the adoption, or was they just gonna keep us around like animals in a zoo?* And of course, *do all the grown-ups think me and Rache are brother and sister? 'Cause we sure don't look alike.*

I was standing there with all these dumb questions like a moron but Rache's brain was quick as ever. "It's a lot to take in."

Pastor Brian nodded. "It sure is."

"Is it alright?" she asked, and she put a little catch in her voice. "Is it alright if J.T. and I go outside for a minute? To get ahold of ourselves, I mean?"

Pastor Brian's face took on a look of concern. "Oh, of course, come with me." He led us through the knots of people in the hallway and out the front door. "Take a couple minutes out here by yourselves. But be back in five, okay? The service is going to start soon."

"Thank you, Brian," Rache said solemnly. "We appreciate it."

The front door hadn't swung closed before we was in the parking lot and on the run. We didn't get more'n ten yards before the front door opened back up and three quick claps echoed through the cars. "Hey! Where do y'all think you're going?"

Don't look back, I told myself. *Whatever you do, don't look back*. I never suspected it would be Rache who did it, though. But she did. For one little second, she turned her head, slowed her step. Maybe there was still some little part of her that wanted to be a good girl who did what she was told. I don't know. But that second was enough to mess it up, 'cause of course she tripped over her own feet and skidded to the pavement. Caught herself with her hands and I helped her up. She wasn't too banged up, clapped off the dust. Didn't even rip that beautiful dress. But sure enough, we missed our chance, 'cause here come Mizz Belinda running across that pure black asphalt in her hot pink high heels.

"Son of a bitch," Rache said under her breath.

"There you two are. What are y'all doing out here?"

"I wanted to get something out of the van I forgot," Rache said.

"What's that?" Mizz Belinda's voice was flat, as if she didn't really believe it.

"My…lucky bandanna. I forgot it in there earlier."

"You can get it later."

"Plus, it's stuffy in there with all those people," I added.

"We needed some air," Rache said.

"Fine," Mizz Belinda said. "You got some air. Now come on." She grabbed Rache's arm and pulled her along. Rache kind of cried out. "Shush it." A hard glance my direction. "And you stay right in back of us."

It struck me, it wasn't me Mizz Belinda had ahold of. I could've gone for it. But without Rache, why bother? There wasn't nothing to do but go back in.

Everybody was just sitting down. The sanctuary was like a big auditorium, and the seats wasn't wooden pews like a regular church, but white folding chairs with speckled cushions. All the preachers was on stage at the front—Jim and Brian and a couple others I didn't know—and there also a pretty kick-ass band, actually, with drums and keyboards and electric guitar and everything. Mizz Belinda and all the kids sat in the first two rows, which I guess the preacher's family has to.

I sat next to Rache in the second row, and while we sang the first hymn, with the lyrics posted up big on a screen above the stage so everybody could read 'em, Rache showed me her arm. It had four bloody marks on it. "That's where she grabbed me with her fingernails," she whispered.

Those marks made me mad 'cause that was Mizz Belinda's spite—she didn't have to dig in like that. I stood up for the songs like everybody else but I didn't sing, even though the music wasn't too bad, as far as church music goes. After that, Pastor Jim gave the sermon, and it was obvious we was in for a long one, so I settled in my seat.

I was thinking at first how I could take a nap without nobody noticing, but the story Pastor Jim was preaching on was one I liked so I started listening despite myself. He preached on how this one kid named Joseph lived in the desert with all his eleven brothers, and 'cause Joseph was the youngest one his Daddy loved him best of all and gave him a coat of many colors. When his brothers saw that, they took Joseph out in the desert to kill him, but when they was about to do it, a caravan came by, so instead they sold him as a slave. To explain what happened, they took the coat and tore it up and rubbed it in goat blood, so their Daddy'd think a wild beast got Joseph.

Now like I said before, this church got all these little sayings posted on the walls, just Bible phrases by themselves about faith and goodness and abide with me and whatnot. I think when people in that church hear a story, they got to make it fit into one of those phrases on the wall, whether it makes sense for the story or not. So Pastor Jim thought this story was all about love, and how the brothers' jealousy spoiled the great love of their daddy, but later on Joseph's love for his brothers overcame it all despite their mistakes, and God's love for everybody turned the mistake around so it was part of his plan and it was all just love, love, love.

I couldn't stand that bull.

I wasn't going to stand up at first, I truly wasn't. But I looked around and I saw all those folks up in that church nodding along, in their beautiful nice clothes, with Pastor Jim up there telling how it was, although it was all lies. And I thought about him and Mizz Belinda intending to adopt me and Rache without even asking us, like it wasn't even a question if we wanted to be part of the lie of his happy house, and I saw all those smug folks nodding along at the lies, and I wanted to stuff the truth in their faces.

So I did it. I stood right up while Pastor Jim was going on and said, loud enough for everyone to turn and look, "That ain't it."

Pastor Jim's head snapped back a bit from the microphone and his eyes widened in surprise. "Excuse me?"

Rache was tugging at the sleeve of my button-down shirt and Mizz Belinda hissed "Sit down" at me but I didn't pay no attention. "You said Joseph's daddy gave him that fancy coat 'cause he loved him so much, and his brothers was jealous 'cause they didn't understand there's enough love for everybody. But that ain't it at all. Joseph's daddy gave him the coat 'cause there wasn't no money."

Pastor Jim chuckled a bit into the microphone. "I'm always glad to see when the young people take an interest in the sermons." There was some laughing in the audience, but I could tell they was nervous. The air was tense with people waiting to see what happened next. "Okay, J.T. Explain it for us."

"Joseph's daddy wasn't stupid. You make it sound like he didn't know what was going to happen when he gave him that coat. But how's he gonna give one kid something fancy like that and none of the others and think nothing would happen? He knowed all the time Joseph's brothers would hate him. That's why he did it."

"Interesting," Pastor Jim said. "Go on."

"Okay. Think about it. There was twelve brothers, and Joseph was the youngest of 'em, right? And the family only got so much money or goats or sheep or whatever they had. How much you think was gonna be left by the time Joseph was grown up, after eleven brothers getting their share? Nothin', that's how much. His daddy had to make Joseph's brothers hate him and drive him out, so he would go someplace new and find hisself his own deal in life."

"But J.T.," Pastor Jim said. "Didn't you listen? When he thought Joseph was dead, his father tore off his clothes and wore sackcloth when the brothers brought the coat back. That doesn't sound like a man who knew his son was still alive, does it?"

I waved my hand. "That was all for show. I mean, sure he was sad 'cause his favorite son left. But all that tearing his clothes off and wearing sacks? It's too much, ain't it? He did that exactly so no one would think it was the way he'd planned it all along. But it was. He knowed his son wasn't dead." And then I sat down, 'cause I'd said all there was to say on that topic.

"Out of the mouths of babes." Pastor Jim gestured in my direction, and the audience laughed again. The tension was broken now and Pastor Jim went on with his preaching like nothing had happened. But the whole rest of the service, Ramon glared at me from his seat. And I should've glared right back, but I was feeling too full of myself to care about him. That was a big mistake. Always stare back.

Chapter Seventeen

That was one frustrating ride home for me and Rache. We'd messed up our chance to run for it and there hadn't been another all morning. We'd been so close in the parking lot—if only Mizz Belinda hadn't called out when she did. If only Rache hadn't… No. Thinking about it won't get you nothing but a cry-cry, as Granny would say. We was tired of it and ready to go, that's all. We'd have to wait 'til next Sunday for another trip to church, unless something else came up.

All the others chitchatted away on the ride home, playing checkers, ready to go eat lunch, but me and Rache just sat in the conversion van's cushiony back seat next to each other, glum and silent. I asked in her a low tone if she was all right.

"So stupid." She shook her head. "Next time, we don't stop for anything. No matter what." And that was all she had to say for the rest of the ride.

Back in the barn, I was waiting my turn to clean up in the bathroom for lunch. Ramon walked by, caught me off guard with a quick gut punch. He got me good too, boy. I was doubled over and thought I might puke right there. But I couldn't let him know it.

"That it?" I gasped. "I been hit… harder'n that… by a girl." And it was true, by Rache. Just as I was getting back up, he cuffed me on the side of the head, knocked me to the floor. Worst of all, the leather pouch fell out of the waistband of my new pants and slid across the tiles.

"Hey, you leave him alone," Hyun-Soo shouted, and jumped on Ramon's back. I was glad he did, 'cause it gave me a second to reach out and grab the pouch. I got my fingers across it, only for Ramon's shoe to step on top.

"What's that?" He shook Hyun-Soo off and sent him tumbling.

"Nothin'. Family pictures. You wouldn't care."

"I tell you if I care." He put the weight down on his

foot. I didn't let go. He pressed harder until I cried out and my fingers spread without my wanting 'em to. He kicked the bag away and snatched it up before I could scramble over.

I was on my feet in a hurry and jumping for it but Ramon held the bag over his head and unzipped it. He pulled out the pictures and thumbed through them and let out a whistle. In a different situation I might've laughed, 'cause that was the exact same thing Rache had done when she'd seen them pictures.

Hyun-Soo was back on his feet again and rammed himself into Ramon, wrapping his arms around his waist and driving him back to the door, right where Pastor Jim was walking in.

"Whoa, what's happening in here?" Pastor Jim asked.

Me and Hyun-Soo and Ramon started talking at once and it was all mixed up until Pastor Jim held up his hand. "One at a time, boys. Ramon, tell me what's going on."

"I walk in here and J.T. and Hyun-Soo jus' attack me. I think they upset 'cause I tell 'em clean up a little. And also, J.T. have a bag with these pictures in it." He held the pouch and the pictures out to Pastor Jim.

"You liar!" I shouted and ran right at Ramon but this time it was Pastor Jim who reached out and put a hand on my head, his arm long enough to hold me back without my swinging arms reaching him.

"Hold on now, son. Just calm down." I breathed in hard but stopped swinging. He drew his hand back and shuffled through the pictures. "Oh, J.T. These aren't appropriate at all. Where did you get these?"

"That's none of your damn business." I made a swipe for 'em but he was faster than me.

"Okay, it's obvious you need to settle down before we can discuss this." He shook his head and sighed at what a shame it was he had to do what he was about to do. "You can spend some time in the closet until you're ready. You too, Hyun-Soo."

Hyun-Soo's eyes got big. "No, I no want to go in closet."

But it was too late. Pastor Jim had me by the shoulder and Ramon had Hyun-Soo and they marched us into the house. I kept an eye out for a chance to grab the photos back but no luck. The closet turned out to be in a spare bedroom on the second floor. I went in by myself with a last hard glare but Hyun-Soo cried and stamped his feet and Ramon had to shove him in. The door slammed behind us and the lock clicked and of course we was in the complete dark. Hyun-Soo beat against the door and bawled.

There was enough room for me to sit against the wall with my legs straight out but not much more, winter coats or something hanging down around my head. At least the floor was carpeted so it was pretty soft.

I waited 'til Hyun-Soo stopped blubbering. I had a question I'd been wondering about. "Why'd you help me out back there?"

"Ramon a bully." He sniffled. "I no like him."

"But he wasn't bullying you. You didn't have to help."

"He bully you now. Before he bully me. No is matter. Bully both ways."

I nodded, not that he could see me in the dark. I let a few minutes pass, idly fingered the fur lining of a coat next to my ear. "You been in here before, huh?"

"Yeah."

"How long they keep us in here?"

"All day."

"What about lunchtime?"

"I think it better if you ate big breakfast." Hyun-Soo laughed a little and I did too. "Tonight I go with you."

"Yeah, soon as we get this door open."

"No. With girl. You go with girl, leave house, never come back?"

"Yeah," I admitted. "How'd you know that?"

"I watch you. You and her. Your eyes always search, search for right time. How you go?"

"We have a canoe."

"Canoe?"

"You know, it's like a little boat. But it can only hold two people."

"I small. I come with you. I no can stand Pink Lady anymore. Or Pastor Jim. They crazy."

I inched my way across the floor and walked my feet up the wall until I was lying on my back with my feet straight up. I reached my arms up to see if I could touch the bottom of the clothes. "So if you hate it here, how come you never left before?"

"I not big. You and girl big."

"We're not that big."

"You big enough."

I smiled to myself. I hoped we were big enough.

It was tough to tell how much time was passing in the total dark, with the only sound our breathing. It actually wasn't too bad in there, once you got used to it. Nice and warm, everything soft, nothing to do so you can kind of go blank. Maybe it's how babies feel before they're born. How long was we in there? An hour? At some point though I realized I had a really pressing problem. "Hey. Hyun-Soo?"

"Yeah?"

"What do you do in here when you have to pee?"

Hyun-Soo laughed and laughed at that. "I show you. Stand up!"

I did and he pulled me by the hand to the back of the closet. "You go that corner." He tapped the corner.

"You mean just pee right here?" He laughed so hard I knowed he meant it, so I pulled my pants down and let it go. I hadn't gone since before church and man, it felt good as anything. The little rumble as the stream sprayed the back wall didn't hurt either.

"Now my turn."

When we were done, we positioned ourselves sitting with our legs across each other so neither of us would have to sit back where we'd wet the carpet. We chatted a little after that, about Hyun-Soo and how he'd come to America from Korea, lived here about six months. Other than the house and the church, he'd hardly seen anything. No outside school, no TV. Pastor Jim and Mizz Belinda hadn't taken him nowhere. I didn't ask him about his family or nothing. Figgered they hadn't brought him here 'cause all that was going good for him.

And then we was quiet again. Stillness, breathing, the occasional growl from our bellies to let us know they was empty. No sounds out in the bedroom. I wondered about that. All the extra rooms in this house, and Pastor Jim and Mizz Belinda had all the kids crammed in a couple barns out back. What was all this space for? Maybe they was saving it for their own kids if they ever had any. I think I dozed off for a bit.

The silence made it real obvious when somebody came into the bedroom outside, even if they was trying not to make noise. Couldn't stop the creaking of the floor, though. I didn't figger Pastor Jim would feel the need to sneak in, so when the door opened it wasn't much of a surprise to see Rache there.

"Nice to see you," I said. "How'd you know we was here?"

"You weren't at lunch so I knew there was a problem. I've never seen you miss a meal before."

"You got me there," I said. "How'd you sneak past Jim and Belinda?"

"They're gone, I think. At least, I heard the garage door open and close. So I came searching for you. And Fatima'd told me how she got the closet treatment once, so I had a good idea where you might be."

"They didn't lock the outside doors?" I asked.

"Sure they did. But all you got to do with those sliding glass doors is jerk up real hard. You know that." Rache pinched her nose. "Goddamn it stinks! Did one of you pee in there?"

Hyun-Soo laughed hysterically at that while I hopped up and sauntered out. "We both did."

"Y'all're disgusting!"

"Hey, when you have to go, you have to go." I opened the hallway door and looked out. No sign of anybody.

"What do you think?" Rache said. "Should we make a run for it now? Do you think we can find our way back?"

"Can't yet," I said. "Pastor Jim took the pictures. We have to find them first."

Rache's face turned sour. "Damn it, J.T.! Why'd you let him see 'em?"

"I didn't want to!" I said. "The pouch fell out when Ramon was knocking me around."

"All right." Rache sighed. "They're probably in the office I saw downstairs."

But we checked the office, me and Rache and Hyun-Soo too, and they wasn't nowhere in there. Not in any of the piles of bills and papers on top of the desk or any of its drawers, not even the bottom locked drawer we found the hidden key to in about three seconds, although there was a bottle of bourbon in there I bet Mizz Belinda didn't know about. We pulled the books out of the wall and paged through 'em and yanked out the leather couch cushions and even emptied the trash can. Nowhere.

"You know what," Rache said. "They might not be in this trash can. But he still might have thrown it away somewhere else. We'll have to check."

"We have to go through all the garbage in the house, now?" I said. Hyun-Soo moaned.

"It could be in there, y'all. We have to look."

So we went through all the cans we could find through the house, dumped out the garbage in the kitchen on the linoleum floor and raked all through it, even the foul meat scraps and greasy napkins and melon rinds runny with sicky-sweet pink juice that released clouds of fruit flies with each poke. At the end we even opened up the bags in the big garbage cans in the garage and rifled through them too. No sign of the pictures or the leather pouch.

"I don't know," Rache said. "I mean, it shouldn't really be hidden, right? He didn't think we'd be looking for it. He must've just put it somewhere we haven't thought of yet."

I flashed back to the locked room I'd found the first day we'd come, the room at the top of the half-staircase I'd seen when I'd gone exploring after taking a shower. "I think I might know where it is," I said. "But I'll have to jimmy the lock."

Rache pulled a hairpin out from her hair and

handed to me. "What are we waiting for then?"

It didn't take me more than a minute to do it once we got up there. The door swung open and I switched on the light and the three of us gasped.

The room was full of dollhouses and other toys, as fancy as you can imagine. Dollhouses sat on tables and desks with little dolls posed in fancy little clothes. Cabinets with glass doors full of china dolls. A huge doll castle in one corner, turrets as high as my chest, with doll knights defending a medieval doll princess. A doll cabin in the middle of a doll barnyard with tiny stuffed pigs and cows and chickens. And it wasn't all dolls either—a herd of about a hundred horses galloped along a countertop, a basket overflowed with glittery costumes, and in the middle of the room, a round display case stuffed full of music boxes that'd lit up and started turning when I flipped the light on.

I didn't know if I should look for the pouch or get down on the floor and start playing with it all. "Whose…whose is all this?" I asked.

"Whose do you think?" Rache said.

I shrugged.

"C'mon, J.T. Who else spends her whole life

dressing up her little dolls and gets mad if they don't stay where she puts 'em?"

"Oh, right." It hit me. That's why the kids was in the barns out back. The barns was just two more dollhouses. "Mizz Belinda."

"Pictures in here?" Hyun-Soo asked.

"Probably not," Rache said. A slow smile pulled at the corners of her mouth. "But you know what? They might be. We'll have to go over every inch."

She started pulling furniture and people out of the nearest dollhouse, which looked like one of those townhouses they have up in New York with its own elevator and everything. Little couches and tables went flying. "Nope, not in there. C'mon, you two. Give me some help."

Me and Hyun-Soo grinned at each other and plunged in. I checked out the herd of horses. Once I knocked that first horse down all the rest tipped like dominoes. At the doll castle, I swooped in like a dragon and laid waste. I think it was more fun than if we'd actually played with it all. I glanced at Hyun-Soo and he was ripping open the clothes in the costume basket so the buttons flew off like popcorn. I saw

Rache at a cabinet of China dolls and called out, "What if the pictures are inside one of 'em?"

"You make a good point, J.T.," she said, pulling out a doll and smashing its face against the floor. She checked inside. "Not in that one."

By the time we was done, the room looked like a trailer park after a twister. I mean, there wasn't nothing left intact, except the twirling display case of music boxes in the middle. I guess we left it for last on purpose, knowing it'd be the main event, but at first we couldn't find a way to get it open. The glass door on the side had a lock built in. I poked at it with Rache's hairpin for a while but I had to walk around while it was spinning and I couldn't make it work. "We'll have to turn off the light," I said.

"Screw that," Rache said. "I've got my own way in." She grabbed a heavy piece of wood that'd propped one of the dollhouses into position and swung it like a baseball bat at the case. Her first blow shook the whole thing, but it held. Her second blow spiderwebbed the glass across one side. Her third shattered the whole thing, and the shards spilled to the floor like a waterfall. We reached in while it spun and pulled all the music boxes out, ripping 'em open and throwing them aside.

There was a weird kind of gurgling sound from the door. We flipped around. Mizz Belinda stood there with her mouth hung open. She didn't seem so hot pink to me now. More a pale pink, like a faded rose. A high-pitch whimper dribbled out her mouth. And when her air ran out and the whimper died, there was still the tinkling of all those music boxes as they winded down.

Chapter Eighteen

Pastor Jim drove his black BMW 730i about ninety miles an hour along those twisty roads, hands so tight around the wheel he could've ripped it right off the steering column. I remembered the last call he'd made before leaving the house: "Hi Brian, thank you for calling me back... You've already gotten there? Good... Yes, I'm bringing them now... Just get everything set up and I'll tell you more when I get there."

Me, Rache, and Hyun-Soo was in the backseat, Ramon in the passenger seat. Rache looked out the window with a faint smile on her lips. Hyun-Soo fiddled nonstop with his fingers and kept his head down. I don't know how Ramon managed to glare at the rest of us without even looking backwards, but he did.

"So we're going to church?" I asked when the phone call was done.

"Yes, J.T., we're going to church." Pastor Jim's tone was mild like he was explaining about the weather. "I didn't understand before, but I see it now. It's so clear. Why the Lord delivered you to us. Rebellion. Strife. Destruction of property. False prophesy. Licentiousness. You two are full of demons. And the Lord sent you to me to cast them out."

I didn't know what to say that, so I didn't say nothing. I tried to think about what demons would feel like, having 'em in you. Would it be like when Mama'd been pregnant with Robby and she'd let me lay my hand on her belly and feel him kick? I didn't feel nothing kicking inside me, though.

At the church, Pastor Jim and Ramon marched us into a little side chapel I hadn't seen before. Pastor Brian was already in there, clearing away folding chairs so there was an open circle in the middle and lighting candles all around, dozens of 'em.

This chapel didn't have none of those silly sayings

on the wall, only a big crucifix with Jesus hanging with thorns on his head and wearing some raggedy pants. He looked out of place there, half-naked and bloody in that room as beige and carpeted as the rest of the church. He looked real somehow, and everything else was fake, the only real thing in that whole place.

Pastor Jim parked Rache and Hyun-Soo on a couple of those folding chairs in the circle, and they put me on one in the middle of it all. I guess Pastor Jim figgered I was the ringleader somehow. Somebody turned out the lights so the candles was the only light in there. Pastor Jim and Pastor Brian put their hands on my shoulders and Ramon hovered around too, but he didn't put his hands on me. Pastor Jim led with a prayer.

"Lord, thank you for bringing this child to us, for delivering him into our hands, so we can cast out the demons that have afflicted his soul. Thank you, God, for your goodness and mercy, that all us sinners can find salvation in your sight if we trust in Jesus. Lord, please bring your power down on us, make your presence felt in this room to drive out the evil spirits here. We call out to you, Lord Jesus, to empty this child of the evil spirits and fill him up with your Holy Love."

That's just a sample really, I couldn't tell you what all Pastor Jim said 'cause he went on for quite a while, with Pastor Brian backing him with "Amen" this or "Yes Lord" that. They were getting into it, and I sat there and looked up at Jesus at the wall, candlelight flickering on his face, staring back at me with his sad old eyes, like he knowed what I had to go through.

I didn't know what I was supposed to do so I sat quiet and let it go on. That must not have been too satisfactory for Pastor Jim 'cause after a while he trailed off and said, "Go and get it, and bring it back, would you, Brian? You know what I mean." Pastor Brian nodded and left. Ramon took a seat in a back corner.

"How long is this going to go on?" Rache asked from her folding chair. "Can I get something to read?"

"Of course you can, Rache." Pastor Jim handed her a Bible from a stack on a table. "You could try Mark 3:11."

"I like reading about Moses," Rache said.

"Why is that?" he asked.

"Because he escapes from Pharaoh, who's not letting the people leave."

Pastor Jim smiled with his thin lips. "I see. And you feel like I'm Pharaoh, by keeping you here?"

"Yes, I do. But don't be too proud of yourself. I've known bigger Pharaohs than you."

Pastor Brian came back in the room and he was holding the leather pouch.

"That's mine," I said. "Give it back to me."

Pastor Jim got excited. "Oh, he reacts! That got them going, I see."

"I don't got demons in me," I said. "I just hate it when people steal something that don't belong to them."

"Brian, bring that over and put it on a chair, would you? That's good, right there in front of us. Not too close." And with that, Pastor Jim and Pastor Brian went at it again with the praying and the hands and everything, louder now than before. After a little while, Pastor Jim unzipped the bag and removed the photo on top, praying the whole time, and he tore that picture into little pieces right in front of me.

"Hey!" I shouted, and tried to stand up, but Ramon

had moved back around and he and Pastor Brian kept me in my seat. I spied Hyun-Soo and Rache out of the corner of my eye. They was sitting and watching, Hyun-Soo fidgety nervous in his chair, Rache stiff in hers with an expression like she was burning up, but what could she do? I had to give her a chance to do something. But what?

And then I knowed. I'd put on a little show. Pastor Jim wanted demons? I'd give him a barrel of demons.

"Holy shit, what're you doing?" I hollered, and flipped the chair backwards. Ramon and Brian wasn't expecting me to go in that direction and I managed to kick the chair away with a big clang even as I landed hard on my back. I actually hit my head on the floor which kind of dazed me for a moment, but I think that was good 'cause when I opened my eyes they musta looked crazy. I thrashed around on the floor screaming out whatever cusses I could come up with, "I'll take you to hell with me, shitheads" and like that.

Ramon and Brian fell to their knees on the floor to hold me down and I snarled and bit at 'em and let spit run down my chin and whip around my cheeks. I tried to pretend like I was a mad dog or a cobra and was getting pretty into it. I mean, I was pissed about the pictures plus my head really was throbbing from banging against the floor so it wasn't all acting, neither. When I saw Rache quietly rise out of her seat I went into overdrive and just closed my eyes and screamed, let it all out, kicked with my one free leg and caught something soft. Somebody, I think Brian, went "oof!" and I kept on wailing and squirming and cussing to give Rache more time. I believe I was at "suck my dick, wiener dogs," when Pastor Jim said, "Hold on. The door's open. Where'd the girl go?"

I couldn't stop now, not when she might be getting away. The toppled folding chair was still nearby and I managed to grab a leg of it with one hand and fling it as hard as I could, no idea where.

"Ow!" And I saw on the edge of my vision Hyun-Soo grabbing his knee and rolling on the floor. I felt pretty bad about that so I did stop, panting for real and keeping my eyes crazy for fake.

"Enough, J.T.," Pastor Jim said. "That will be quite enough." He tapped Brian on the elbow and pointed to the door. "Go look for the girl." He knelt beside Hyun-Soo. "What's wrong? Are you okay?"

Hyun-Soo shook his head. "Knee hurt. I try walk." He limped a few steps and his leg buckled under him. He tumbled to the ground with a little cry.

"Okay, okay," Pastor Jim said. He helped him up. "Can you stand on it?"

Hyun-Soo stood and his leg held. "Yes. I think so." When Pastor Jim looked away for a second, Hyun-Soo gave me a wink.

"Right. Why don't you sit here? We need to get some ice on this." Pastor Jim turned to me, still sitting on the floor. "J.T., we'll have to continue in a few minutes. Come have a seat next to Hyun-Soo."

I didn't move, and Ramon kicked me in the small of my back. "Get movin', demon boy."

I went and didn't complain. The chair where Pastor Jim had left the leather bag was empty. I smiled to myself. None of the adults seemed to notice it was gone, and that meant all I had to do was get to the canoe, any way I could.

"Ramon, go to the kitchen and get a bag of ice for me, would you?" Pastor Jim said. "You remember where the Ziploc bags are?"

Ramon nodded and left. Pastor Jim picked up a

Bible and sat in a seat near the door.

I picked up the Bible Rache had left on a chair and pretended to read it. It didn't take too long before Pastor Jim was intent on some passage or other. That's what I was hoping for. Maybe Hyun-Soo and I could make a break for it. But I didn't really see how. He'd spot us well before we got to the door. The idea I had next made me wonder if I really did have demons in me.

What was it Granny'd said about God looking the other way if a starving man steal an apple? I sure hoped God was looking the other way now. I quietly picked up a candle from the seat next to me and held it under the Bible 'til it caught.

"Hey, what are you doing?" Pastor Jim said. "Knock it off!"

But he was too late. The Bible was flaring up and I tossed it on the stack of other Bibles. Pastor Jim ran over and tried to blow it out but the flames was already too high by the time he got over there. I guess those thin little pages burned pretty good. He started unbuttoning his shirt, shouting behind us, "Ramon! Ramon! Come back! Forget the ice!" while Hyun-Soo and I took off for the door.

I knowed we couldn't head for the canoe at first 'cause there was no telling how close Pastor Jim or Ramon was behind us. They could burst out the door any time. So I led me and Hyun-Soo into the trees, but away from the canoe, on the other side of the church. Once you got outside the mowed area right around the building, the trees and things was pretty thick, and it wasn't no trouble to find us a little indented area in the ground behind some bushes. That's where Hyun-Soo and I sat tight.

Ramon and Pastor Jim did come out of the church, Pastor Jim's shirt covered in black scorch marks. He called our names as they went, Rache's name, Brian's name. Nobody answered. Ramon didn't say a word but kept a couple steps behind him. They went off into the parking lot and I didn't see where after that.

I waited a few more minutes but it seemed safe so I tapped Hyun-Soo on the shoulder and we made our way around to the river, going real quiet and slow and taking care to avoid the brambles. And there was the canoe, right where me and Rache'd left it on the riverbank, and seeing it was like seeing your house again after being gone a week. I checked inside and there was the backpack, only somebody'd opened it, and all our gear was spread out over the seats and floor. I didn't see nothing missing from what I could tell, but still, Rache was gonna be pissed about that.

Speaking of which, where was she? She'd escaped first, she should be here by now. Maybe Pastor Brian had caught her. But I couldn't think about that.

While I stood there trying to figger about Rache, a big raindrop hit me right in the forehead, and another on my arm a second afterwards. "Great," I muttered. "C'mon, Hyun-Soo, let's wait under that big tree out of the rain."

Before we could move, somebody stepped out from behind the trunk of the very tree I'd been looking at. Between it being almost evening, and the storm clouds, and the shade of the tree, I couldn't see who it was at first. Me and Hyun-Soo didn't move.

"Who are you?" I called out.

The figure didn't speak but took a step forward. It was Ramon, and the junkyard could've used the look he gave me to cut scrap metal.

We had a staring contest for a minute across the

grass, the rain starting to come down heavier now, wetting my hair and dripping down the back of my neck. Without breaking the stare he came over, punching one fist into an open hand, tramped right into my personal space, my eyes only up to his chin. "What the hell do you want?" I said.

"You remember what I tol' you?" His purple scar looked like a little snake slithering down his cheek as he worked his jaw.

"No. Why would I care about anything you say?"

He shoved me hard and I stumbled back a few steps and fell on my butt, but I bounced back up again. "You shoulda listened," he said, and took a swing at me I saw coming from a mile away. I ducked and caught him with a fast punch in his leg.

By now he was all up on me, though, and we tumbled down into the cold muddy grass and rolled around side by side. 'Course he was bigger and if he got on top I was through, so I folded my lower leg back and dug in to keep him from pushing me over, all the time hitting him wherever I could with my free hand—in his chest, his arm, his neck. He couldn't even fend my fist off 'cause he was mainly trying to flip me on my back with *his* free hand, which like I said, I was preventing with my leg, plus I was pretty slick from the rain and his hand kept slipping off.

We was breathing so hard our hot breaths was in each other's faces and our clothes was sticking to our bodies and our hands was sliding over our skin as we grappled. He caught my shirt and tried to yank me over but all the buttons popped off. So much for my new dress shirt. I reached up to try to thump him one in the ear but that was a mistake 'cause it meant I had to unlock my leg. He heaved and landed his body weight on top of me, putting both hands on my face and pushing my head down. I could feel my hair squish into the mud.

"What'd I tol' you?" Ramon said as he started to pummel me. "I said, don' fuck things up for us." A blow to one cheek. "I said, things is good here." The other cheek. "But you got to fuck it up." Bop on my nose, and the blood started running. "You don' know nothing. You don' what it's like bein' hungry."

"I been hungry," I said through gritted teeth. "I know what it's like."

Ramon dug one knee into my chest. "Not like me,

you don'." He pulled his fist back and I knowed I was about to be hurting. The blood from my nose was already hot and iron-smelling on my upper lip.

A hand from somewhere grabbed his fist and kept it from plunging down. "Ramon, stop!" Pastor Jim's voice.

But Ramon didn't. He was still on top with one knee grinding into my chest, and Pastor Jim tried to pull him away but Ramon slipped free and got his hands around my throat and squeezed. I could feel his thumbs crushing in the soft part at the front and his fingers, tightening around the cords in my neck. It got real hard to breathe.

Then something metallic clicked. "All y'all. Stop right now." Rache's voice.

I couldn't move my head but out the corner of my eye I could see: Rache held a silver gun with both hands and pointed it straight at Ramon.

Chapter Nineteen

"Okay, Rache," Pastor Jim said. "Stay calm now."

"I'm very calm," she said.

I didn't doubt it. Her hands was steady like she was holding a toothbrush.

"And y'all need to back off of J.T."

"C'mon, Ramon," Pastor Jim said. "Do what she says."

The fingers loosened around my neck and the pressure of Ramon's knee came off my chest. I gulped in a huge breath.

"Step back," Rache said. Ramon and Pastor Jim moved back. "More steps. Keep going." Without moving her head her eyes scanned the area. "Stand up, J.T."

I turned over on my stomach and pushed myself up out of the cold mud. Rache had a plastic grocery bag by her feet and wet hair hung in her face. I couldn't stop a shiver, shaking streams of rainwater from my body. My left leg ached as I rose. "Boy, am I glad to see—"

"You don't talk either, J.T." She edged slowly toward me, leaving the grocery bag behind but keeping the gun on Ramon. "Hyun-Soo, come over and stand by us."

"Wait a minute now," Pastor Jim said. "We don't know if Hyun-Soo wants to go with you. We have to ask him."

"Ask him then," Rache said.

"Well, Hyun-Soo? Do you really want to go with them? Think about it. When J.T. and Rache showed up, they hadn't eaten in days. Do you want to risk going hungry?"

Hyun-Soo looked from me to Pastor Jim and back.

Pastor Jim went on, his preacher's voice creamy as peanut butter. "Think how frightening it would be not to have a place to go home to. Always running away, and never able to stay in one place."

He still didn't move. But he was listening.

"And always getting in trouble. That might be the worst part. So much trouble you have to use a gun to get out of it. It might seem like fun at first, but I think you'd get tired of that kind of life pretty fast."

I wanted to protest, to say the way he was describing it wasn't fair, but I couldn't. It was pretty much the truth. Hyun-Soo shook from the choice he had to make and his eyes went back and forth, back and forth.

"I…I so sorry," he finally said. He went over to Pastor Jim's and Ramon's side.

"There's your answer," Pastor Jim said.

"Fine. J.T., grab that plastic bag over there," Rache said. I picked it up and something clanged inside. "Go put it in the canoe and push the canoe in the river and hold it there. Nobody else move."

As I followed Rache's instructions I realized my left leg was really hurting. I mean, not sure I should be walking on it hurting. Each step sent tingling pain up the back of my thigh and across my left butt cheek. But I didn't want to show it right then. I winced on the inside until I reached the canoe.

Rache took baby steps toward me, pointing the gun the whole time. She carefully stepped in the canoe and took a seat, never lowering her arms. "Now J.T.'s going to get in this boat and we're going to float away. If I see anybody move before we're out of sight, I'm shooting. Do you hear me?"

"We hear you, Rache," Pastor Jim said. "You go ahead."

"J.T., climb on in," Rache said.

I did, ignoring my leg, and that's how we got down the river. Rache aimed the gun until they was out of sight while rain slapped the gray plastic canoe frame with pelting sounds, hard little hits that split each drop into a thousand tiny droplets, spattering and soaking all our stuff. Finally, she let her arms fall.

"Thank goodness," she said. "That sucker's heavy."

"Can I hold it?" I said.

"No." She put the gun on the seat beside her.

"Why not?"

She rolled her eyes and pulled the leather bag out from her waistband. "What you need to do is to put this away."

"Oh, I almost forgot about that," I said.

"Not me." She handed it over and I slipped it in my own waistband where it belonged.

We drifted for a while, getting soaked straight through, but not daring to stop. Rache packed up some of the things in the backpack to get them out of the rain. The gun, the cooking gear, a few other items. The plastic shopping bag.

"What's in that bag, anyway?" I asked.

"Food I got in the church pantry."

"I'm glad to hear that," I said. "I'm starved."

Rache laughed. "All that just happened and all you care about is food?"

"Hey, I didn't get lunch!"

"That's true." Rache pushed her wet hair out of her face. "I guess we should think about stopping soon and setting up the tent."

"Yeah," I said. "It's too late to keep our stuff dry. I bet you're pissed at whoever messed it all up."

"I did it," Rache said.

"You did? Really?"

"I had to get the gun out and it was at the bottom of the backpack."

"It's not like you not to do it nice and neat," I said.

"I didn't have time! Too busy heading back to the church to rescue you, as usual."

That got my dander up. "I didn't need no rescuing. Me and Hyun-Soo found our own way out."

"I guess so," Rache said.

"You know so."

"Anyway, there was nobody there when I got back and the whole room was full of smoke."

I decided it'd be best to keep quiet about the Bible burning. Rache could be funny about things like that. "So what'd you do then?"

"I went to the kitchen and filled the bag up, then came out and found you getting your head pounded in, *as usual.*"

"Yeah, about that." I stretched my left leg out and turned it from side to side, trying to figure out which ways made it hurt. "I think I pulled something wrasslin' with Ramon."

"Your leg?"

"Yeah, here on the back of it. Up all around my hip, too."

"We really need to stop then," she said. "Get you rested."

The rain was letting up a bit. I wiped a hunk of mud from a fold in my ruined dress pants and flicked it into the river. And to think they'd been new just that morning. But I was stalling. I had one thing I was burning up to ask.

"Rache?"

"Yeah?"

"Would you really have shot Ramon?"

"I don't know," she said. Silent a second. "Probably."

I nodded. Of course, there was one last person we hadn't talked about. "So. Whatever happened to Pastor Brian?"

"Huh." She thought a minute. "I dropped him early on and never did see him again. Maybe he got lost in the woods."

"He might still be out there wandering around!" I said. We hooted about that. I pictured clueless Pastor Brian in the trees somewhere, still trying to figger his way back to church.

* * *

We found a grassy field by the river that seemed like a good spot. It was almost dark now so we was eager to get the tent set up, but once we'd grounded the canoe, my leg and hip was hurting too much to help Rache set things up. I could barely climb out of the canoe actually, had to let my right leg do almost all the work.

I held out the flashlight where she was working, which was about all I could do. I felt bad, but Rache told me don't strain myself, we'd go to sleep and see how it felt in the morning.

Inside the tent we stripped down to our underwear but didn't want to keep the dripping clothes in the tent. Rache went out and hung our things from a tree branch. We figgered if it rained it'd wash off the mud, and if it didn't they'd dry off. I opened up the grocery bag to see what dinner was. Hungry as I was, I almost didn't have the appetite for what I found.

Rache unzipped the tent flap and I held it up. "A loaf of bread. And Spam."

"Is Spam not good?" she asked as she climbed in.

"Ain't you never had it?"

"Nope."

"Well, I guess you're gonna find out." I held up a

can and shone the flashlight on it. "Teriyaki flavor. Six cans of it."

"I didn't have a lot of time," Rache said. "I was just tossing in what I saw."

"Couldn't you have seen some Oreos?"

"Hey, I didn't see you showing up at the canoe with groceries!"

I handed her a slice of wheat bread with a nice thick Spam wedge. She put it to her lips and took a little nibble.

"It's…not too bad."

"If you say so." I shook my head and ate my own Spam sandwich. I was pretty hungry but I decided one sandwich was enough. By now it was completely dark out so we unrolled the sleeping bags. They was damp on the outside, like everything, but dry enough on the inside. Still, it was too warm and humid in the tent so we had our arms and legs flung out all akilter. Rache's hand brushed mine and she grabbed it and squeezed it.

"You know you make me feel safe," she said.

I goggled at that. "You feel safe around me? Like you said, I'm the one you're always rescuing."

"You rescue me plenty. And if you weren't here, I'd

be all alone."

"You wouldn't be here at all," I said. "You came with me 'cause I was running away. Don't you remember? Without me, you'd be feeling even safer in your own bed back home."

"You're wrong," she said. "That's the last place I'd feel safe."

We didn't talk after that, but she kept her soft hand in mine. The rain drummed a beat on the walls of the tent. I wondered if Jerry liked this kind of weather. Maybe he played along with it. I hoped the old man at the bait shop wasn't still ripping him off, and Jerry letting him for the sake of being friends. After a while Rache's hand relaxed and her breathing turned slow and regular. I waited a few minutes more so I could be sure she was really out.

"And you make me feel like I can be somebody important," I whispered.

* * *

Throughout that night the rain pounded our little tent like we was Noah's ark, and the next day wasn't no different. We might get a breather here and there when it'd let up for a bit, but it was always threatening, and afterwards it'd start in worse than ever. Other than pee breaks we stayed inside the tent all day, which was fine with me since my leg still hurt. It got boring as hell after a while.

What did we have to eat? What do you think? Spam sandwiches for breakfast. Spam sandwiches for lunch. And for dinner, bread with a side of Spam. And we was still only on the second can. Four more to go.

"Hyun-Soo don't know what he's missing," I said as I chewed one of them sandwiches. "More for us, I guess."

"Ugh," Rache said. "Maybe I should've joined him."

At one point in the afternoon we'd actually gone about an hour without rain so Rache went out to get our clothes from the tree branch. "They're not too wet," she yelled. "Plus, I think your pants are almost clean."

"Great," I yelled back. I was pawing through the backpack, looking for something.

She handed my pants and shirt to me through the tent flap. She'd already put on her dandelion yellow dress. "These is still awful damp," I said while she climbed in. "How come yours is already dry?"

"I think it's a thinner material."

When she'd sat down, I pulled the gun out from where I'd hidden it under my sleeping bag and pointed it at her. "Bang!"

Her face turned white. "J.T., put that down right now, and I am not messing around."

I turned the gun over in my hands, ran my finger over the bumpy black plastic on the grip, along the cold smooth length of the barrel. "Geez, Rache, it was just a joke."

"Not a funny one. Not funny at all." She held out her hand. "Give it to me."

"How come you didn't tell me you had this, anyway?"

"This is exactly why. Boys can't handle things like this. Now give me the damn gun."

I passed it to her and she carefully laid it in the bottom of the backpack. I knowed she was mad from her jaw, how it was all tight and made her cheeks push out. "I like your dress," I said.

"Shut up."

She didn't talk again after that for a long time. I went out to pee. My leg wasn't quite as sore now but I was still limping. After, I stood in my underwear outside and just looked around. Gray skies, drooping tree branches, the dark slow water of the river so smooth you almost wondered if it wasn't really glass. But then that smooth surface started getting spotted, and the rain drops hit cold on my bare skin, so I went back in the tent.

Our dinner Spam loosened her lips and she was willing to speak again. We laughed about Mizz Belinda's face after she found us in her dollhouse room, how after her gurgling she'd managed to stumble to the top of the stairs. We roared each time we repeated her words. "Get up here, Jim," she'd said all breathy. "I need you to get up here now." She hadn't even been willing to look at us in our faces until Pastor Jim came running full steam up the steps. Ah, it'd been great.

"Rache, can I ask you a question and you won't get mad?" I asked.

"How can I promise that when I don't know the question yet?" she said.

"I just want to make sure you don't get mad for no

reason," I said. "'Cause I got an innocent question, but I don't want to you take it the wrong way."

She gave me a look. "Just ask your question, J.T."

"Where did the gun come from?"

"Oh, that," she said. "The drawer in Laban's bedside table. I took it when I packed up before meeting you at Granny's."

"How'd you know it was there?"

"It was always in there, from the day we moved in after the wedding."

I laughed. "What, you was already going through Laban's drawers on the first day?"

Rache nodded. "That's right. I never trusted that rat bastard. Not from the first second I saw him. Soon as he and Mama went to the store I went through everything in the whole house."

"What else you find?"

"Just the gun. I'd check on it every few days. Only one time I checked the drawer and it wasn't there."

"Oh yeah? When was that?"

"Strangely enough, it was the night before we ran away. And then it was back the next morning."

"Huh," I said. "That's weird."

The rain finally quit sometime after it got dark. That wasn't a real restful night. Not having done nothing all day, our bodies didn't think it was time to go to bed. We didn't hold hands, either. Eventually we fell asleep but the sleep was weak and our dreams was bad.

* * *

"Knock, knock."

Something thumped twice against the side of the tent. I blinked my eyes open. Birds singing, sunshine already bright. Some god-awful putrid smell and I realized it was my Spam breath after sleeping all night.

Two more thumps. "Good morning! You know y'all are trespassing, right?"

Chapter Twenty

I unzipped the flap and stuck my head outside. A dark-skinned man sat on top of a horse. He was linebacker-sized—huge-shouldered, giant gut, but he smiled when he saw me. "Hi, son. Tell your daddy I want to talk with him."

"My daddy ain't here."

"Your mama then."

"She ain't here either."

"Fine. Your uncle, your granddaddy, I don't care. Tell whoever's in there to come out."

"Rache, someone wants to talk to you."

Rache stuck her head out too. "Yes, sir?"

"C'mon, enough fooling, kids. Where's your parents?"

"It's just us," Rache said. "We're camping out."

"Your parents know you're—"

"No, they don't know we're out here," Rache said. "We didn't tell 'em."

"And we ain't going back," I said.

"Well," the man said. He scratched his chin. "That makes it straightforward." He shifted down off the horse, a shaggy brown one with a white patch around its right eye. "Don't make it easy, but it makes it straightforward. How long y'all planning on camping here?"

"We're breaking camp soon as we wake up," Rache said. "And since you woke us up, I guess that's now."

"Where you headed after that?" the man asked.

"We're canoeing down to Wilmington."

"Wilmington?" the man said. "Shoot, I can drive y'all there if you want. Save you some time."

"Really? Is it far?" I asked.

"In my truck, half an hour." The man pointed at the river. "In your canoe, probably half a day or more."

Rache and I glanced at each other. We were almost there. But could we trust this guy? Rache nodded.

"We'll take that ride," I said.

"Okay. Who you got waiting for you down there?" the man asked.

"A friend of the family," Rache said.

"Mm-hmm. They expectin' you?"

"No," Rache said. "But I know she'll be happy to see us."

"You sure about that?" When neither of us answered, the man squatted down and peeked in the tent. "What've y'all got to eat for breakfast in there?"

"Spam," I said. "We can make you a Spam sandwich if you want."

"Ha, no thank you. How about I make you something instead? And then give you that ride?" He held out his hand. "We got a deal?"

I was ready to shake but Rache pushed my hand down. "Not yet. J.T.'s hurt his leg, so wherever we go, he needs to ride your horse."

"You got it, young lady," the man said with a laugh. And this time I did shake his hand, and Rache did too. "J.T. and Rache, ain't it? My name's Mr. Henry, by the way."

We started rolling up our sleeping bags and Mr. Henry got himself back up to a standing position with a long groan. I don't think his knees liked pushing up that huge gut of his. I liked him, though, and I was kind of excited 'cause I'd never ridden a horse before.

Fortunately, we done it enough times by now we could pack the tent and things in a real hurry. And then Mr. Henry helped me up on top of his horse, who was a girl horse named Elohie. It wasn't no trouble sitting in the saddle, and I believe Elohie hardly noticed I was up there after carrying Mr. Henry. I scratched her fur between her ears, not silky like a dog or cat but rough almost like pine straw, and Rache petted her nose, which she seemed to like. Mr. Henry gave Rache a sugarcube to feed to Elohie, which she definitely liked, just took it right out Rache's palm and rolled it into her mouth with her big pink-gray horse tongue. I kinda wished I could feed Elohie too but I didn't say a word 'cause I was the one getting to ride her and Rache had arranged that for me.

"How far is it to your house?" Rache asked as we set off.

"Not far, not far," Mr. Henry said. He walked in front on a little trail and Elohie followed with her head bobbing up and down. "This here's my two hundred acres. I gotta walk it every morning."

"Why do you gotta do that?" I asked.

"See there ain't no kids trespassin', like today." Mr. Henry laughed at his own joke. I didn't know if the joke was too funny but it was hard not to laugh along with him 'cause it was a real deep low-down laugh that came from his whole body.

The trail came out of the pine trees and we passed by a field of tall leafy plants lined up in between dirt rows. Little greenish-gray bunches hung off the plants.

"What're those?" I asked.

"Blueberries," Mr. Henry said.

"They don't look like blueberries."

"That's what they look before they ripen. They'll get blue, don't worry."

"Are you a farmer?" Rache said.

"We do blueberries on fifty acres," Mr. Henry said. "I wish we could do more. My daddy farmed tobacco, but that ain't steady like it used to be. Unfortunately, I got to work at the paper mill to keep the money comin' in. I been thinking about putting in a crop of Christmas trees, though."

"You mean you can grow Christmas trees, like corn

or something?" I said.

Another deep laugh. "Of course! You don't think those guys you see selling Christmas trees just go out in the woods and start chopping, do you?"

"I never even thought about it before," I said.

Mr. Henry was right about the distance 'cause we was already there, a two-story white house with a bunch of muddy old cars and trucks and parts out front. Even the trucks that was up on blocks and some tires and rusty axles and so on was arranged in a neat order, though, and the grass was mowed and the gravel driveway didn't spill out its path. Mr. Henry helped me down off Elohie and slapped her backside, and she walked off to a pen next to the house.

"Ain't you scared she gonna run off?" I asked.

"Who, Elohie? She my girl, she ain't goin' nowhere. Now set your stuff down on the porch and come on in and meet my other girls. Maybe the boys too, if they can tear themselves away from their videos."

Inside the house smelled unbelievably good and I knowed we was in for some real breakfast. Mr. Henry bellowed out, "Mama, come on out here."

"I'm frying up the ham," came the call back. "We almost ready to eat."

"This is more important. Come on out!"

A woman nearly as big as Mr. Henry came out of the kitchen with an oven mitt in one hand and a spatula in the other. Her huge, um… bosom filled an over-sized t-shirt that said *Luther Vandross Tour 1988.* "Darryl, I swear to God—" She stopped short and looked us over. "Well, you didn't say we had guests."

"Some kids camping out by the river," Mr. Henry said. "I brung 'em in for breakfast. Kids, this here's my wife. E'erbody call her Mama Henry."

I thought maybe I'd hold out my hand for a handshake but Mama Henry was hugging us both before we knowed it, never mind her hands being full. She practically smothered us in that bosom of hers and smelled all like coffee and bacon. "Well, come on in to the table, y'all. I get Dinelle set two new places." She called up the stairs. "Dinelle, come down and set two more places at the table! We got visitors!"

"They headed down to Wilmington," Mr. Henry said as we went back to the dining room. "I'm gonna give 'em a ride after we eat."

"I hope you put some gas in the truck yesterday when you come home from work, like I told you to," Mama Henry said.

"Don't you worry about it," Mr. Henry said. "You mind your part, I got mine under control."

In the dining room, the long rectangular table was loaded. I mean, biscuits with gravy, grits, sausages and bacon, and I intended to eat so much I'd never have to taste a Spam sandwich again in my life. And then a girl who must've been Dinelle came in with a couple plates under one arm and silverware in her other hand.

Dinelle was tall and wore tight jeans and a white t-shirt. She was 'bout as pretty as I seen, and that ain't no lie. Long black hair in curls below her shoulders. Light brown skin, eyes like caramels. I don't think I ever seen anything like those eyes. I guess I must've studied on 'em for a minute, 'cause the next thing I heard was Rache clearing her throat.

"And this here's J.T.," she said. "I don't know what's wrong with him."

"How old are you?" I asked Dinelle.

"Fifteen," she said.

Rache punched me in my kidney. "Hey! What's that

for?"

"Wake up, dummy. It's time to sit for breakfast."

I waited 'til Dinelle sat at her place and tried to take the seat next to her but somebody pulled on the back of my t-shirt and I couldn't walk. I flipped around and it was Rache, pointing at the seat next to her.

Mama Henry brought in pitchers of syrup and little butter plates and pulled her seat out at the opposite end from her husband. "Where's the twins?"

"Playing video games, as usual," Dinelle said.

"Darryl, would you?" she asked.

"Don't make me come back there!" Darryl shouted.

"Now I could have done that myself," Mama Henry said. "I meant go tell them."

Mr. Henry left the room but it hardly mattered 'cause his voice shook the house. "It's breakfast time and I'll turn that thing right off, so if y'all want your saves you'd better be out here in a hurry!"

A scrambling from somewhere in back the house and two boys bounded in, and I bet a bear would think twice before wrassling with 'em. They was kinda like smaller versions of Mr. and Mrs. Henry, though I don't think they was much older than us. They took their seats next to their sister without hardly looking at me and Rache.

"Boys, be polite and introduce yourselves to our guests," Mama Henry said.

"Hi, I'm Jayden," one said as he reached for the plate of pancakes.

"Jaylen," the other said, already grabbing the bacon tongs.

"Put those hands down," Mr. Henry said. "Y'all know to wait for grace."

I sighed on the inside, expecting a long time before we could eat. But actually Mr. Henry said a few easy words and then it was over. Nothing fancy to show off with, like a few people I could name. We all said "Amen" and started in, and if I thought I was hungry, I never seen nobody eat like those twins. Pancakes and scrambled eggs, biscuits and ham slices went in like they was popping jelly beans, all washed down with enough coffee to take a bath in. Beforehand, I would've said there was twice as much food as we needed, but that table was cleared to the bones by the time we finished.

I made sure I got my share too though, especially

of the pancakes, which of course was packed with blueberries. I wasn't too eager about the coffee, 'cause I wasn't never allowed to drink it at home. I guess it wasn't too bad, though it was kind of bitter. Everything else made up for it though.

"Can we help you clean up?" Rache asked Mama Henry afterwards, which I wouldn't have suggested myself, but I had to admit the Henrys done us good.

"Oh, honey, you're too sweet," Mama Henry said. "Why don't y'all take your plates to the sink, and then Mr. Henry can check if that truck of his'll start."

"I hear you in there, Mama!" he called from the next room.

I couldn't hardly walk outside my stomach was so full and Rache held her hand on her belly and groaned. "Too much!" she whispered to me.

In the driveway, it was tough to tell what worked from what didn't. We probably wouldn't even have gone to the right vehicle if Mr. Henry wasn't right in front of us. The truck he walked up to might've been white at one time, but it was so covered with mud and dust you could hardly tell. The back of it said it was a F-R-D.

We popped our gear in the bed and climbed in the cab, with Rache in the middle. The seat was a big plastic bench with a rip across it and all the stuffing welling out. Mr. Henry turned the key and the engine whined a bit and turned over. We pulled out and bounced down the gravel driveway to the paved road. We couldn't've gone more than half a mile when there was a sound like a gunshot and the whole truck shuddered and rolled slowly to a stop.

"Well, shoot," Mr. Henry said under his breath. "I really shoulda put in five bucks' worth yesterday."

Chapter Twenty-One

We sat in the truck for a couple minutes after that with nobody speaking. I knowed why. Mr. Henry didn't want to walk back and go tell Mama Henry how the truck conked out. But there was nothing else to do.

"C'mon, kids," he said. "Let's go back. We'll try again later."

When we got to the house, Mama Henry was at the sink with her arms in soapy water up to the elbows. She didn't seem too surprised at the news. "Why don't you call that brother of yours and see if he can do something useful, for once?"

Mr. Henry was already dialing the number in the phone on the wall. He held it up to his ear for a minute. "Not answering."

"Of course not," Mama Henry said. "He probably been out drinkin' and fightin' 'til all hours."

"You know Darnell ain't that bad," Mr. Henry said.

"We'll just see if he come through this time," Mama Henry said. "Well, take the kids back and see if Jayden and Jaylen'll let 'em have a game."

In the den, the twins was playing Madden Football on a Sega Genesis in front of a huge-screen television. Me and Rache sat in overstuffed chairs while they was on a couch, arguing and cursing the whole time.

"You're going down, mofo!" one twin said when his Panthers sacked the other's team's quarterback.

On the next play, the Saints quarterback made a pass for fifty yards in response. "Ooh! Ooh! The long bomb! Watcha gonna do about that, huh?" The other twin jumped up and shuffled in a circle.

"Sit your ass down, son. You're still down fourteen points. All you gotta do is make that pass about ten more times."

"Watch me!" The next pass sailed clean but the man guarding the receiver jumped at the last moment and caught it.

"Oh! Interception! Interception!" The first twin put

his hand to his forehead and faked fainting off the couch. "Damn, bitch, you didn't have to make it so easy for me."

And so on for probably twenty minutes. I didn't mind sitting, with my leg tired after the walk on the roadway, and I watched the twins careful until I could tell 'em apart. Jayden was a bit taller, his hair closer cropped, and one of his eyes had a twitch in it when he got excited. Jaylen was quicker to smile, his hair grown out slightly. Or was it the other way around?

I don't know if the twins realized we was in the same room. Me and Rache sure didn't get a chance to play, but I wouldn't've wanted to get caught in the middle anyway. A couple times I thought they was even gonna get physical, start punching each other right there on the couch, but they always calmed it back down just in time.

Mr. Henry came back in. "Okay, my brother's gonna be by about noon with a gas can, if you two kids want to sit tight until then."

Me and Rache glanced at each other. She leaned over the arm of her chair and whispered, "Shouldn't we be going?"

"But we might still get there faster if we wait. With my leg and all."

She raised her eyebrows but didn't disagree. "We'll wait," she said to Mr. Henry.

"I'm glad to hear it. In the meantime, y'all oughta get out in the fresh air." Mr. Henry snapped off the television and pointed at the twins. "I mean, all y'all."

Jayden and Jaylen stared back at him with mouths hanging open. "That ain't fair! We was in the middle of a game!"

"I don't want to hear it. Outside. Fresh air." Mr. Henry went out the door. "And get your sister on the way out too. She don't need to be on her phone all day, neither."

***

The five of us walked down some dirt trail headed the opposite direction from the river. "Where're we going?" I asked.

"The 'hood," Jayden said. He and his brother could hardly take three steps without one bumping, tripping, or tackling the other.

"The branch on that pine tree," Jaylen said, pointing ahead.

Jayden nodded. "Yep." And they took off to see who could jump highest to tag the branch with his hand.

"What's the 'hood?" Rache said to Dinelle.

"There's a few houses down this way," Dinelle said. "That's just what we call it."

As we walked, we heard a crack followed a moment later by a softer thump. The sound repeated itself a minute later. Rache perked up at the same time as the twins. It was the sound of a baseball hit by a bat and landing in a mitt.

"C'mon," the twins said to me and Dinelle. "Let's move."

I tried speeding up my limp. "I can't go no faster."

"You too slow with your leg," Jaylen said. "Climb on my back."

"What?"

"Come on, you skinny," he said. "Climb on."

"You can't carry me there," I said. It was true, about how skinny I was. I could see it in my arms especially. They hadn't been that skinny before the canoe trip. I glanced at Dinelle, though. I didn't want to look like I couldn't do something simple in front of her. "You're big but you can't carry me."

That must've been the wrong way to put it 'cause Jaylen got all put out. "I can do it! You don't know me. Climb on, I'll show you." I didn't like it but I have to admit it was faster. I kept my legs wrapped around his midsection and my arms on his shoulders and Jaylen hardly bent over. Not as easy for him to carry me as for Elohie, but not too far off.

The trail passed through a grove of pines and came out in an alley behind some houses with fenced-in yards. The yard with the noises had a tall wooden fence, wild mulberry trees and vines all overgrowing it. Jaylen let me down and we went in through a place where the wood had caved in and nobody ever fixed it.

Inside, there was a pretty big yard behind a two-story house with several boys and a few girls playing baseball, from probably eight or nine years old up to about the twins' age, plus one older teenager maybe sixteen. Jayden and Jaylen took charge right away, dissolving the old teams and picking new ones, with them the team captains. Jaylen picked me and Rache together at the end, ahead of the little kids, but that's about it. 'Course if they'd knowed about Rache she'd've been a first pick, but everybody always underestimates her 'cause she's a girl. Their loss.

The older teenager waved 'em off when they was picking and stood off in the shade with Dinelle. She was whispering something to him in his ear he was laughing about. He had dark skin and jug ears and a wispy mustache. His laugh sounded fake to me and he leaned in to her, like he was trying to put his arm around her, and if I saw it right away I knowed the twins did too.

"Which team you on, Shaquille?" Jaylen said to him. "I let you pitch, if you want to."

"Naw, little man," Shaquille said. "I'm good. Y'all go ahead without me."

"Little man?" Jaylen said under his breath. Louder, "You know my sister ain't going out with no ugly pooch like you."

"She ain't interested in no big-eared baboon," Jayden said.

Shaquille gave them the finger as he whispered something back to her. She giggled over it and didn't pay no mind to her brothers. The twins both clicked their tongues but we started playing anyway. First base was a baseball glove, second a piece of broken-off pavement, and third an old tree stump. Home was an actual home plate that I think belonged to a t-ball stand except somebody ripped off the tee.

Like I said, me and Rache was on Jaylen's team, along with two boys named Brayden and Jesse and a couple younger kids. Jaylen pitched, of course, and before we even started he threw the ball at me, hard, with no warning. I caught it and glared at him. "What the hell is that for?"

"Good hands," he said. "You play first. That way you won't have to run on your leg." He put Rache on the left side to play third/left fielder, Brayden in the middle to play second/center, and Jesse behind the plate as catcher. Little kids could slot in wherever. We turned out not half-bad, 'cause Jayden's team got a couple hits but they didn't score nobody, and I caught all the throws to first without no mistakes. Then it was our turn up to bat.

Brayden struck out, Jesse got a hit and made it to first, and Rache was up next in the batting order.

Jayden threw a soft one by her but it was too high. Soon as I saw he was slow-pitching her I knowed what would happen. The next one was right where she wanted it and she nailed it so hard the crack from the bat sounded like a tree branch breaking off. The ball bulleted straight past Jayden and would've kept on going if it hadn't thunked against the fence.

"Dayum," Jayden said, pounding his fist in his glove. One of the little kids ran back to try find the ball in the vines while Jesse and Rache trotted around the bases.

Jaylen gave Rache a high-five as she crossed home plate. He was laughing so hard he could hardly stay upright. "You just got your ass handed to you by a girl, bro!" he called to Jayden. "You didn't even try to catch it!"

"I didn't wanna lose my hand," Jayden yelled back. "Looks like you got yourself a ringer."

When I got up to bat I actually got a nice little hit through the gap between a couple kids up the right side but I couldn't hardly limp my way to first base. "Run! Run, you crip!" Jaylen hollered but it didn't help me move any faster. Even trying to run made my leg hurt even more, and they threw me out. That was it for our side and Jaylen shook his head and jutted his jaw out as he ran out to the pitcher's spot.

We'd played three innings and Jaylen's team was beating Jayden's seven to two. It was pretty clear Rache was the secret ingredient, with a hard hit every time she came up to bat, but we was also better in the field, with Rache and Brayden hardly letting nothing get by and firing 'em to me at first, where I reeled 'em in. Jayden got madder and madder as the game went on, cussing out his players when they didn't get on base or dropped a ball in the outfield. We was up to bat and when even one of the little kids got a hit Jayden's eyelid started twitching so bad I thought he might burst a vein in his head.

"Goddammit!" he screamed at the outfielder who'd let the ball go past, an eight-year old with big eyes. "Can't nobody here catch a ball? Why didn't you run at it?"

"Why didn't you?" the kid sassed back, and now it seemed like Jayden was about to melt down.

But for some reason he stopped short. He didn't say a word. He glanced around the field. He called to

Jaylen, real calm and sing-song, "Where Dinelle at?"

"What?" Jaylen said.

Jayden slammed the glove to the ground. "Dinelle, you dumbass! She ain't out here."

"And Shaquille gone too," Jaylen said, catching some of his brother's mood.

"They went in the house," Rache said.

"How long they been in there?" Jayden said.

Rache shook her head. "A while ago. Maybe fifteen minutes."

"And you didn't say nothing?" Jaylen said.

"What for?" Rache said. "I thought maybe they were getting something to drink."

Jayden and Jaylen stood near each in the field, Jayden flexing and unflexing his fists, his right eyelid twitching absolute crazy, Jaylen pounding the end of a wooden bat against a rock. It was like they was working up each other's agitation without even talking, each just making the other furious, feeding off each other.

At some point, Jayden nodded darkly and that was the signal for them to stride to the back door. Jaylen didn't drop the bat. All the other kids hung back, not wanting to risk getting involved. Me and Rache glanced at each other. Not even a choice for us. We followed fast as my leg allowed.

The back door held 'em up a bit 'cause it was locked, but Jaylen smashed the window with the bat and reached through.

"Hey, y'all," Rache said. "Let's slow down a second."

They didn't slow down. They was in the house and through the kitchen and up the stairs, us behind 'em fast as we could. In the upstairs hallway, all dark from the closed bedroom doors, it wasn't no mystery where Shaquille and Dinelle was. Boy and girl moanin' came from one bedroom at the end of the hall. Jayden slammed the door open so hard all the pictures hanging in the hall fell to the floor and shattered.

Shaquille looked up from the bed where he was under the covers but on top of Dinelle, their clothes spread across the floor. "What the fuck's going on?" he said.

"Jaylen? Jayden?" Dinelle tried to pull a sheet across her bare chest. "Go back outside. We busy in here."

The twins met each other's eyes. "Don't it burn you up?" Jaylen said.

"Our sister and this big-eared baboon," Jayden said. "I can't stand it."

Shaquille had noticed the bat and was stumbling out of the bed now, his hand over his privates. The irritation on his face had turned to fear. "C'mon, y'all. Your sister wanted—"

Jaylen drove the knob of the bat up against Shaquille's chin. Shaquille's head snapped back and he stood there a moment like he was suspended in the air, one hand still covering himself, the other reaching out to us with fingers spread, his eyes rolled back in his skull so they was complete white. His body crumpled like an empty grocery bag and hit the floor.

Chapter Twenty-Two

Shaquille was right at my feet. His body gave one big twitch that crabbed him all up, then relaxed. I bent down to take a look.

"Is…is he okay?" Jaylen asked. All the fight seemed drained out of him and his brother.

"No, he ain't okay," I said. Shaquille was taking in fast, shallow little breaths and his face had a thick shine of sweat over it. "At least he's breathing, I guess."

Jayden picked up his sister's clothes and tossed them at her. "Put these on. Let's get out of here."

"He don't look right," I said. "We need to do something to help him."

"What you want to do?" Jayden said. "If he

breathing, he be fine."

"We should call an ambulance or something," I said.

"No!" Jayden said. "We don't need no ambulances. They bring the cops with 'em. He all right."

I looked up to Rache for help.

"He's probably in shock," she said. "Dinelle, hand me a blanket off that bed. At least we can cover him up. And the pillows too. We need to elevate his feet." She was already on her knees arranging things. She nodded at me. "J.T., you go make that call."

"Hey!" Jayden stomped his foot. "I said no ambulances."

Rache gave him a look like a viper. "All right, J.T., don't tell them what happened. Come up with a story, say there was an accident or something."

I limped my way downstairs and found a phone in the kitchen. I explained to the lady at nine-one-one where in the house Shaquille was laying and that he'd fallen and hit his head. I answered some questions about his condition and whatnot and when she asked the address I remembered my trick of using a piece of mail and gave it to her. She told me to stay on the line until the ambulance arrived but the others was coming down the stairs so I hung up. Strange, I'd never called nine-one-one in my life and now I'd done it twice on our trip so far.

Outside, all the kids in the yard was kind of circled up around the door but when we came out they took one look at our faces and scattered in every direction. They knowed something bad had happened and didn't want to be anywhere near.

It was a quiet walk to the house, with Dinelle hanging behind even my slow-ass limp, sniffling every now and then. Jaylen and Jayden was in front, stony and cold. They didn't run to jump up and touch any branches this time.

"He was asking for it, though," Jayden said at one point.

"He was not," Rache said. "He and Dinelle weren't hurting anybody. You two are hotheads."

"He got what was coming to him," Jaylen answered, as if Rache wasn't even there.

In the gravel driveway, the twins turned around. "None of y'all is breathing a word of this to Daddy or Mama," Jayden said. "Got it?"

Me and Rache and Dinelle didn't talk back, which I guess they took as agreement. They went off behind the house somewhere and Dinelle trudged up to the front door. Me and Rache wasn't real sure what to do and kind of hovered around the old car parts. Mr. Henry came out the front door after a few minutes.

"Everything all right?" he asked.

I shrugged and Rache toed her shoe in the dirt. I hated to keep the truth in but didn't see what Mr. Henry could do about it now, anyway. But if Mr. Henry noticed we was unwilling to talk he didn't show it.

"Well, bad news, kids." Mr. Henry put his giant hands on our shoulders. "My brother never came by and it's almost one o'clock. But I do have a favor to ask of y'all."

"What's that?" I said.

"I wonder if y'all could give me a lift in your canoe?"

Rache had a half-smile on her face, like she wasn't sure he was serious. "But Mr. Henry, I don't know if our canoe is, well…"

"You're scared I'll swamp it, ain't you?" A deep

belly laugh.

Rache's half-smile became a grin. "Well, yeah."

"We just have to see," Mr. Henry said. "But we really got to try it 'cause otherwise I got a six mile walk to the mill and I be late fo' sure. I figger on the canoe it should cut my time by more'n half."

We fetched our stuff at the porch and Mama Henry came out and hugged us one last time and gave us sack lunches while Mr. Henry brought Elohie around. The nice thing about Mr. Henry's plan was I got to ride her again, which I really needed 'cause the back of my thigh was aching hard after the baseball game and all that.

Elohie seemed happy to clop along with me and the gear on her back, bobbing head, ears swiveling when they heard something but otherwise unbothered by the rest of the world. Her life was simple, walking along or eating grass and being content. No worries about who done what or where you got to be on time or who got to know the truth about something. Her truth was grass and sky and trail and that's it.

At the river there was the canoe near where we'd camped all through the rain, and already that seemed like a long time ago. Mr. Henry gave Elohie a clap on her rump and she trotted off for home. When he got in the canoe it sat a lot lower in the water than we was used to, but it didn't sink. We loaded up our gear and climbed in too. He had the middle seat and we was on either end.

"See, no problem!" he said. "So y'all can just drop me off at Highway 210 when we reach the bridge. Should be just about a mile walk from there." He even grabbed one of the paddles and helped speed us on our way.

It was almost funny how close we was to the water, just reach out and splash in it if you wanted to, didn't even have to lean. Mr. Henry pointed out the names of the little islands in the river as we floated by—Bird's Cove Island, and Raccoon Island, and so forth, and he knowed who lived up all the little creeks flowing in the main part of the water and told us their stories. After one of the stories, he was quiet a bit and said, "Yep, you never know what could happen in these parts. Or do y'all disagree?"

He looked from one of us to the other and I got the feeling he might've had more of an idea of what happened earlier with the twins than he was letting on. I was scared to bring it up, 'cause he'd been so nice to us and I didn't want him to get angry.

I glanced at Rache. She chewed her lip a bit. "Mr. Henry, there's something else we need to tell you."

"I had a suspicion you might." Mr. Henry's face darkened. "It's the twins, ain't it? I knew it when I saw 'em slinking off behind the house. What they done now?"

"We was playing baseball in someone's yard," I said. "And Dinelle…and…" I didn't quite know how to explain about her and Shaquille.

"And we had an argument and someone got hurt," Rache said.

"Was they okay?" Mr. Henry said.

"We don't know," I said. "It looked pretty bad. Jaylen hit him in the chin with the end of the baseball bat and he was knocked out cold."

Mr. Henry blew his breath out. "Shoot. Out cold, huh? Who was it?"

"Shaquille," I said.

"Well, I ain't too surprised to hear he was involved. What happened then?"

"I went to the kitchen and called an ambulance."

"What'd the EMTs have to say?"

"We didn't stay," Rache said.

Mr. Henry raised his eyebrows. "Y'all didn't stay when Shaquille was laid out on the ground?"

It sounded pretty cold when he put it like that. "Nobody did," I said, though I knowed that was weak sauce. "All the kids disappeared when they saw there was trouble. Jayden and Jaylen said he had it coming."

Mr. Henry stared off at something on the shore and let the canoe drift a minute. He muttered something I thought sounded like, "They exactly like my brother." Then he shook his head. "Well, I better call up Mama Henry soon as I get to the mill. We ain't heard the last of this."

It was about when we was finishing that conversation when the bridge came in sight. Mr. Henry checked his watch. "One forty-five. I should just make it. I got to thank you kids for this."

"It wasn't no big deal," I said.

Mr. Henry pointed downstream. "Now in about an hour or so, this river's gonna join up with the Cape Fear and the water's gonna spread out. You two need to stay near the shore as much as you can 'cause the Cape Fear got some bad currents sometimes."

"But it's possible to canoe on it?" Rache said.

"Oh, definitely. People do it all the time. Just take care, and if you're lucky you should be in Wilmington before the sun goes down." He pulled a tiny black notebook and a stubby pencil out of his jeans pocket. "Now listen. If your friend ain't there, or something go wrong, you call me. I'm writing down my number for you. Will you promise me you'll do that?"

"We'll do it," I said.

"You promise?"

"We promise."

We let him off and he climbed up the concrete to the road and waved at us from the top. The rest of the way went exactly how he'd said it would. We ate our lunches from Mama Henry, which was meatloaf sandwiches and bags of salt-and-vinegar chips and pieces of blueberry pie and a couple Cokes.

In about an hour the two rivers joined up, the Black River flowing into the Cape Fear River, opening up like going from a residential road to an interstate highway. Even the water color changed, the dark tea of our river spilling in and changing over to the black-green of the Cape Fear. After all this time, we was really and truly almost there.

PART FOUR

Chapter Twenty-Three

There was more and more houses along the shore the farther we got, with their own docks at the river attached to long wooden stairways up to the main house. We saw other boats now on the water too, but if anybody spotted us or cared we couldn't tell. It was pretty late when we crossed under a big highway bridge with tons of cars whooshing by over our heads and after it we caught our first sight of Wilmington. The sun was setting so that light spilled from over the forest on the far side of the Cape Fear onto the jumble of the city, church spires and white stone apartment buildings all jutting up from the brick warehouses and green leafy patches. All along the water ran a wooden walkway with people strolling on it, and riverboats and smaller boats lined up alongside. On the other side of river, set back in its own little cove, a huge blue-gray battleship hulked over the water, spiny looking with antennas and three big guns thrusting off its deck.

"If we was driving that thing, we wouldn't have to worry about the sheriff or Laban," I said to Rache.

"Just blast them to hell," she said.

We found an empty place along the wooden walkway and paddled the canoe underneath, figgering there had to be a rope somewhere we could tie up to. We kind of maneuvered under there in the green slime and bobbing soda bottles and cigarette butts, ducking down to make our way through wooden beams, all while folks was walking overhead, not even aware anybody was below them. Finally we did find a rope and tied it up. We climbed up out of there and over the top of the framework like lizards on the side of a house, surprising an old man with his elbows on the railing, staring at the water.

"Excuse me, mister, do you know where Duchess Street is?" Rache asked when he turned to stare at us.

He pointed at a busy street full of people mingling and going in and out of storefronts. "Go up Market

Street, turn right anywhere y'all want. Duchess's about five blocks down."

"Thanks, mister," I said.

"Y'all kids all right?" he asked.

"Sure," Rache said. "We just gotta get home before dinnertime."

We strode up into Market Street as nonchalantly as we could, but I had that feeling like I'd had back at Pastor Jim's, realizing all of a sudden how long it'd been since we'd washed our clothes or had a shower. The streets was all brick and there was flag decorations hanging everywhere 'cause of course it was almost July fourth, though it was hard to believe we'd been on the river that long. There was an ice cream shop with families setting on benches outside and I asked Rache, "You still got your twenty-seven dollars?"

"We're almost there, J.T. We can't stop now."

"Yeah, but I'm hungry."

"Yeah," she said, and she stopped and stood on the brick a minute. "I am too." She glanced over at the ice cream shop and in her eyes she was wanting it as much as me. "Okay, we'll stop, but only for a little while."

The air conditioning was on so hard in the ice cream store that you could feel the cold blowing out as you walked up to the door, and inside the freezers was all buzzing loud. Waiting in line was a killer 'cause there was two parents and three kids ahead of us, and they couldn't make up their minds. Well, that was fine for them, 'cause I bet they was there as an after-dinner treat, but for me and Rache, this was all we'd had since our sack lunches. Although I had to admit, there was a lot of flavors to choose from.

I got a cone with pistachio, which I'd heard kids talk about at school but never tasted myself, and it turned out to be green but still pretty tasty. Rache got rocky road like we'd had back at the lake house, and we sat on a wooden bench separated by a tree from the other benches and ate and traded bites so we could each try the other's flavor. And when we was done we throwed away our napkins and went on to Duchess Street.

It wasn't no problem finding it, once you went down Market Street a ways and turned right. The stores disappeared and it was all these historical houses, spaced real close together, with big old front porches held up by pillars and some of 'em with stone walls around the front yard. Once we was on Duchess though, we didn't know the address, and it turned out to be a long street. I wasn't real sure we'd ever find it, either, since the sun had set now and it was getting pretty dim.

We wandered up and down in front of those houses for a while and finally got directions from an old lady walking a poodle. "Excuse me, ma'am? Do you know where Ms. Gardiner lives?" Rache asked her, and it struck me I'd never even known the name of this friend before.

"Lucille Gardiner?" the old lady repeated, and Rache nodded. And it turns out we was lucky, 'cause she said, "Why, she's in the house on that corner," and pointed to a powder yellow-painted house with red shutters and brick stairs up to a porch covered with potted ferns and flowers. The front door was red too, with a stained glass window in it but it didn't show a church scene, just a sort of pattern of blue and yellow rectangles and circles.

Rache knocked on the door and when nobody came, a second time, louder. We heard steps inside and the porch light flipped on and the door opened. I guess I expected Ms. Gardiner to be an old lady like the one in the street, but she wasn't, she was a grown-up but younger than Mama or Aunt Marnie. Pretty too, with long wavy brown hair and a smile when she saw us. And there was something familiar about her I couldn't put my finger on.

Rache spoke, and there was a bit of a shake in it. "Ms. Gardiner, do you remember me?"

She peered at us for a moment and then her eyes lit. "Why, Rache, of course I remember you! What are you doing here?"

"I ran away. With my cousin, J.T. Is it okay if we stay here tonight?"

"Oh, my," Ms. Gardiner said. "You two are a long way from home."

"Please, just for one night?"

"Well. Yes, you can stay in the guest room. Please, come in." She gestured for us to enter and took us to a table in the kitchen. Her house was clean, all wooden floors and new appliances. Everything felt fresh, the paint and the furniture and lots and lots of plants. "Can I get you two something to drink, a glass of water or something?"

"Thank you, that'd be great," Rache said.

She and Ms. Gardiner chatted a bit then, about our canoe trip and how long we been gone. I couldn't really pay attention though. I just stared at Ms. Gardiner's head, the side of her face as she got out the glasses and filled them with ice and water from the little spout built into the steel refrigerator. Something about her. I knowed I seen her before, but I couldn't imagine how. Or maybe not her, exactly, maybe a picture of her. But I couldn't think where. Possibly at Rache's house? It was driving me crazy.

"So, are you kids hungry?" she asked as she set the glasses in front of us.

"We had some ice cream on the way over here," Rache said. "We're fine. We actually brought something we hoped you would look at."

"What's that?" she asked, her face really curious. She took the seat across from us.

"J.T., do you want to get out the photographs?" Rache said.

I pulled the pouch from my waistband. The only light was from a lamp over the sink and there was funny shadows all around the room. I dropped the pouch in the middle of the table and Ms. Gardiner picked it up and unzipped it, pulled out the folded-over photos and went through them one by one without saying a word. She nodded and made little "hmm" sounds, flipped some of 'em around or brought 'em up close to look at some detail, but not until she'd gone through them all did she talk.

"I guess you got these from Joe Ammons?" she asked.

Of course that was Big Joe's real name, and I flashed back to his blood and guts, blasted out across his living room, and that raw hamburger smell. I put it out of my mind fast as I could. "How'd you know that?"

"He told me himself, for one thing. That he had enough evidence to bring down everybody in Wyattsville. Said he'd do it someday, too, when he had a mind to. I never believed him, he was too deep in his alcoholism by that point to believe anything he said. But I guess in the end he really did have it."

"So you can use these?" Rache said. "Print them up in your newspaper?"

Ms. Gardiner laughed. "The Morning Star's not really my newspaper, I just work there. I do think my editor would be awfully interested to see these, though. We'd have to talk about what kind of story he'd want to pursue, what angle. There's a lot going on here."

"But you know Big Joe's dead, right?" I said.

Ms. Gardiner breathed out slow. "Yes, I did hear that. I told him for years he should move out, come down here. He never would budge from Wyattsville, though, even after the beating."

"What beating?"

"Oh, he got beaten up pretty bad about ten years ago. Used to be a private investigator, you know. Pretty good one, too. But at some point he started looking into things some real big shots didn't want him looking into. Things like these pictures. Somebody wanted to teach him a lesson, I suppose. After the beating, he walked with the limp. Kind of gave up, I think. He'd always been a hard drinker, but that's when he stopped taking cases and dedicated himself to the bottle like it was his job. Looks from this like he never stopped taking pictures, though. Kind of a romantic figure, when you think about it…" She blinked a couple times and looked at us.

"Is everything okay?" Rache asked.

"I should ask you the same question. You kids look like you could use a shower and a good night's sleep. I know you said you weren't hungry, but how about I make you some soup and then you go get cleaned up? We'll talk more in the morning."

Ms. Gardiner's guest room was perfect, with two single beds and a little nightstand in between, a round corded rug on top of the wood floors. Blurry paintings of stone houses with flowers in window boxes in Europe or someplace on the walls. After we showered the sheets was refreshing cool when you slipped in and then warm before you could shiver.

Without the pouch hidden in my jeans I felt lighter, almost like I could float up and touch the ceiling. Which was silly, 'cause the pictures didn't weigh hardly nothing, but it was the first time in weeks I hadn't had that pouch against my skin. I closed my eyes and I think I was out almost instantly. The last thing I heard was Ms. Gardiner down in the kitchen, talking softly on the phone.

***

My eyes snapped open. Middle of the night, no sound. I knowed all of a sudden where I seen Ms. Gardiner before. I snuck out of bed and down the stairs real quiet. The pictures was still on the kitchen table so I gathered 'em up but it was too dark to make out what was on 'em. I found a place in the living room at the front of the house where the street light shone in and I sat on the floor there and went through each picture one by one.

I was almost through 'em all before I found what I was looking for. It wasn't one of the sexy scenes, but one of the ones with drugs, a group of people passing a little glass pipe. They was in a room somewhere with white painted walls, maybe a bedroom, but it was hard to tell. Laban was there in the middle, face all flushed beefy red, laughing. A couple people with the backs of their heads to the camera. A woman with a real low dress so you could practically see her boobs held the pipe but she was handing it to another woman, a pretty younger woman with wavy brown hair, off to the edge of the picture so you almost couldn't see her, but enough of her face was visible to tell. And my stomach flipped right then 'cause that was Lucille Gardiner.

Chapter Twenty-Four

Rache looked the photo over in the pool of light from a little reading lamp between the two beds in the guest room. Her eyes scanned it again and again before she looked up, her voice low so we didn't wake Ms. Gardiner.

"Are you sure it's her?" Rache asked. "I mean, she looked these pictures over herself and didn't say anything."

"Pretty sure. I think it's 'cause she's off at the edge, you hardly notice her. Maybe she had her thumb on that part."

Rachel studied it hard again and frowned. "Yeah, but she's a reporter? She could've been undercover. Reporters do that when they're working on a story, right?"

"Maybe." I thought she was reaching with that one.

"I know they do, J.T." Her voice wasn't too sure. "I've seen it on TV. That's probably what she was doing there."

"You're right," I said. "Like on TV."

The photo dropped from her fingers. "Goddammit!" She stomped the heel of her foot and ground the picture against the wooden floor.

"Rache, you have to be quiet!" Felt weird for me to be the one saying that. And then some real bad news occurred to me. "You know what? Do you remember Ms. Gardiner talking on the phone last night when we was going to sleep?"

Rache turned a shade paler. "Laban could be here in the morning."

"Yeah," I said. "He could be driving here right now. Sheriff Tate too."

"Get your damn clothes and shoes and socks on, J.T. We're going." She ground her teeth. "And grab the pictures on the way out."

The streets was foggy in the dark and every noise sounded probably three times louder than it really was.

A car driving in the distance. An air-conditioning unit flipping on. The sounds felt like they came out of nowhere, little air pockets under the big blanket of fog, and we pushed our own way through, opening the pocket ahead of us while it collapsed where we just was a moment before.

Rache walked slow so's not to get ahead of my limp, but I knowed she was feeling in a hurry. As we got closer to the riverfront there was some grown-ups laughing behind a building. A bearded man carrying a guitar case came out the mist so quick we almost jumped, but he didn't pay us no mind.

At the wooden walkway Rache leaned over the edge to spot where our canoe was. We had to climb over and through the woodwork down to it. It'd been a lot easier climbing up the day before, and I was afraid one of us'd fall in the water, but Rache made it to the canoe first and steered it over so I could climb in easier.

I guess we didn't know where we was going, but we'd been traveling so long on the river it seemed like the natural place to go. We launched it and paddled into the dark water with ribbons of fog twirling around us. It's not that we forgot about the strong currents in the middle of the river Mr. Henry warned us about, but it didn't feel safe close to the town so we paddled across to the other side, the battleship side, and stuck to the shore over there.

As we floated downstream, there was all these little slips of islands dotted around. They'd come real sudden out of the fog. We came to one that was a curve of trees with some sand around 'em. "Right here," Rache said, and we pushed onto the edge, although the sand turned out to be mixed with mud sucking our feet down.

It was more solid up around the trees so we set up our tent there, in the middle so hopefully nobody could see us. It was already getting a bit light out but we tried to get some sleep. I was tired but there was so many questions. What was we going to do? Where could we go now? I did drift off eventually.

* * *

When I woke up it was full bright day, maybe even afternoon, and Rache was sitting up on top of her sleeping bag with her eyes half-closed. That was a good sign 'cause it meant she was figgering things out. "You get any sleep?" I asked her.

"Yep. A little." Tapped on her knee a few times. "It's no big deal, you know. We can go straight to the newspaper. We won't need Ms. Gardiner."

"Are they gonna take the pictures from a couple kids?"

"Why not? You heard her. She said her editor would be awful interested to see them. She said there's a lot here. We just have to go to the newspaper building and ask to see the editor."

"But what about us? Are we gonna come back here? We can't live out here."

"We'll use a phone at the newspaper office to call Mr. Henry. He told us to call him if we needed to, and I bet we could even stay there a couple days. And after that, after Laban and everybody are in jail, it'll be safe for us to go home."

I liked that idea. Seeing Mr. and Mrs. Henry again, and Dinelle too. Maybe getting to ride Elohie. And after that, Mama and Robby and my house and my room, and a visit to Granny to tell her all we done. But

I put those thoughts out of my mind right quick before I got that sickish feeling. Chickens before they hatch and all.

"Okay," I said. "Let's get across the river and find out where that newspaper is."

"But first, breakfast," Rache said.

I groaned 'cause I knowed what was coming now. "Do we have to?"

"J.T., we have plenty of bread and Spam left and we'll be hungry if we don't. Besides, we shouldn't waste it. Now move your stinky feet so I can get in the backpack."

After breakfast we went out and did our business. I took the pouch out from my waistband and set it next to some dandelions while I squatted for what I had to do. It was later than I thought it'd be, with the sun overhead, shining on the river water so it hurt your eyes to look too long. The air smelled of river but there was a breeze with salt on it, and I remembered Wilmington was close to the ocean. Water lapped up along the sand, and hornets buzzed along the edge, flitting in and out of ferns and things. I got pretty interested, just watching where they was flying, but my little daydream was broke when Rache screamed.

I yanked up my pants and darted over to her spot, tufts of brown grass up to your thigh, and pushed through where she just stood and screamed and pointed, and there, not three feet away, a long snake, tan bands up and down its black-gray body, half-curled, its head raised in the air and black eyes staring hard. This was one time I decided not to stare back. I grabbed Rache's arm but before I could pull her away that snake hinged its mean mouth wide open and inside was ridged light pink along the bottom and cotton white along the sides and there wasn't no doubt: water moccasin.

I yanked Rache away now over to the tent and she was stumbling along like she was in a daze. Not like her to be the panicked one. *Maybe she's just afraid of snakes,* I thought. Couldn't blame her for that. Now that we was away and safe I actually laughed.

"That was a close one," I said. "At least you didn't get bit."

"J.T.," she said, and her voice was hoarse. She pointed at a place on her left calf. There was two dark red marks there about an inch apart, with little drips of watery blood rolling down underneath.

Chapter Twenty-Five

"Oh my God." I couldn't panic. Had to stay calm. Rache needed me now. "What'll we do?"

"We'll follow the plan," she said. "Pack up and take the canoe across. They'll have a first aid kit at the newspaper when we get there."

"Alright," I said. "But you sit down. I'll pack away the tent and everything."

I had the tentpoles out and was breaking 'em down and putting 'em in the bag and the tent had collapsed down like it was letting out a breath. There was some kind of moaning from behind me and I wondered if there was another animal on the island but when I turned around it was Rache, and she had tears running all down her face, which scared me 'cause it was something I never thought I'd see.

"It hurts so much, J.T." She had her leg stretched out and it was starting to get puffy around the bite marks. "It hurts so much."

Screw the tent. I kicked it away unfolded under some bushes and took Rache's hand. "Can you make it to the canoe?"

"I think so."

I hobbled her over and grabbed the backpack on the way. She got her puffy leg over the side and situated herself on a bench. I pushed off and paddled fast as I could for the far shore. I never paddled like that before and it wasn't long before my shoulder was screaming stop and my lungs was pulling fire but every time I looked up Rache was crying.

Oh shit, the pictures. The pouch was still next to the dandelions. We couldn't go to the newspaper without them. Here I'd been carting those damn things halfway across God's earth and I forgot them now? I stopped paddling a second and was about to ask if we should go back but Rache let out a groan. *Who cares about the pictures? We'll come back for 'em later.*

Mr. Henry wasn't wrong about the currents on the

river 'cause once we was in the middle it was speeding us along a lot faster than I expected. When I finally did paddle us over to land we was so far down the shoreline our island was hardly in view anymore. The bank there was pretty steep and probably ten feet high and covered with brambles but it was the same all the way both ways so I jumped out and pushed the canoe up far as I could. It'd be more climbing than walking.

"I don't know if I can make it," Rache said.

"You can." I slipped on the backpack and stepped out and held out my hand from the bank. "I'll help you. It'll be easier once we get to the top."

I pretty much had to pull Rache up the bank, which wasn't so easy 'cause the dirt was sandy, crumbly stuff, and each step up was followed by a slide back down, but eventually we was over and on even ground and she could walk on her own. It was thick piney woods with undergrowth and slow going, but neither of us was in shape for a jog anyway. I went first, pushing through and holding the plants and branches so they didn't slap Rache, who was moaning behind me but that was good, it meant she was keeping up. We came in view of a cinderblock industrial building with a blue roof and I led us towards it.

The building was in the middle of a rough old parking lot by a grassy hill up to the road. The sign by the road read "DeJohn Marine Motors" with a drawing of a speedboat on the water underneath. I looked down and Rache was at the bottom and not coming any farther so I clambered back down.

"You just lay down here." I took off the backpack and put it under her head. "I'll go flag down a car, okay?"

Rache nodded and settled her head on the backpack. It was a pretty nice little area of grass and the sun was going behind some tall pines and was all dappled on the ground there. At the road I paced up and down and kicked gravel on the shoulder and waited probably fifteen minutes for somebody to pass by. *Where is everybody? Where's all the damn cars?*

Back at the bottom Rache had fallen asleep, though she was still moaning. The bite was ugly, her entire left calf all swollen up and the skin pasty-looking, with the area right around the bite itself purple-black. Her face was pale and her hair was shiny wet from sweating. My stomach felt sick with worry looking at her.

Still no cars. Only the cicadas singing in waves getting so loud it'd almost make your ears hurt, then fading back almost to nothing before starting up again. I checked the building out. A couple windows with bars on 'em that you couldn't really see in, and the only door was metal with no knob or handle, just a padlock through a hole in a latch. Air conditioning unit and a dumpster out behind, and a pile of round white rocks in the corner of the parking lot. It was probably just a storage building.

Back up to the road to kick around the gravel some more. What was the deal? Was it Sunday and everybody at home? I tried to remember what day it was but we'd been too long on the river, and I couldn't rightly figger how long we'd been on it. Like that for an hour, two, who knows. Me pacing the road and Rache asleep at the bottom. My stomach growled all the time but I ignored it. How could my stomach growl when Rache needed me?

The light was fading and I sure didn't want us to spend the night out here. Would it be better to go off on my own, back to Ms. Gardiner, the newspaper, a hospital, anywhere really, and send somebody back for Rache? But I didn't want to leave her for that long, either, especially in the dark. I didn't know what to do, where to go, who could help. Finally I closed my eyes and just prayed.

Lord, if you're listening, we could sure use some help. I guess I ain't always been the best-behaved but I ain't asking for me, I'm asking for Rache. If you could help us now I wish you would send a car along or anything. Just please help us out.

I opened my eyes. Cicadas. Sun below the trees. Rache moaning. And a telephone rang in the cinderblock building.

I dashed as fast as my limp would let me. The phone kept ringing. I picked up one of the white rocks, about the size of a cantaloupe, and smashed it against the padlock. Once, twice, and the third time it broke off and the door swung open. Inside there was a single fluorescent light in the back corner, buzzing and flickering over a desk. The walls was dark wood paneling and linoleum floors, and there was all kinds of boat engines up on crates. The desk was covered with papers and that telephone, an office phone with lots of flashing buttons at the bottom but I seen 'em before, you gotta push the button that's lit up and then answer, which I did.

Person hung up right before I picked it up, but that was okay. I stuffed my hand in my pocket and pulled out the crumpled paper with Mr. Henry's number on it. I punched it in and let it ring and ring. Five times. Ten. And thank God, he answered.

"Yello," he said.

"Mr. Henry, it's me, J.T."

"J.T., where you at? What's wrong?"

I told him all about Rache and the snakebite and DeJohn Marine Motors and its address, from a piece of mail, of course. "I be there as fast as I can," he said, and he hung up. After that it occurred to me I could call nine-one-one, but Mr. Henry was on his way. It'd be confusing if he got there and we was already gone. Anyway, he'd be there soon and know what to do. We just had to sit tight.

By the desk there was one of those water machines with a big clear tank on top where you take a plastic cup and push the little white button and you can see the bubbles float up while your cup fills. I drank a cup and it was nice and cold and I filled one to take out to Rache. I shook her awake and she opened her eyes slow, and when I held the cup to her lips she drank it all down. She didn't say nothing but when I asked if she wanted more she nodded so I got her another and brought it back out.

It was pretty much dark by now, except for a streetlight up by the road, and I almost jumped out my skin when I heard an explosion behind me. I was kneeling on the grass with the almost empty cup at Rache's lips and I flipped around and there in the sky, in the direction of the city, was a big circle of glowing red, and a second explosion and blue flares streamed down, and a bunch of crackles and silver lights flashed all across. And of course it hit me, it was the Fourth of July.

I sat down by Rache and laid my head on the backpack by hers and held her hand and squeezed it and she squeezed back and when I looked over her eyes was open and staring up at the show. There was all the explosions and bright flashes, all colors and patterns and booms and whistles for a good half hour, I bet, finishing up with a big finale so the sky was almost like daytime, and when it was over I looked at Rache again to see if she liked it but she was so, so still and I knowed right away.

Chapter Twenty-Six

Mr. Henry's pick-up truck pulled up and I guess he'd finally got some gas in it. He left the headlights on and the motor running while he climbed out. "J.T., there you are. Took a while to find this place and I'm kicking myself now 'cause I should've told you to call an ambulance. How's Rache doing?"

I pointed down at the bottom of the hill but there was nothing to say.

He scrambled down. "Rache, honey, how you feelin'? You ready to go to the hospital? Sweetheart?"

I didn't look, just stood there and watched moths flutter around in the headlight beams. A minute later Mr. Henry was behind me and laying his big hand on my shoulder. We both stood there. The night was sticky and my legs itched but I didn't scratch.

"Why the stack of rocks?" Mr. Henry asked finally.

I wanted to explain. How they was going to come and take her away, and everybody'd forget about what happened. We was only kids, I knowed that. But with that pile of white rocks there maybe somebody'd walk by once in a while and wonder how it got there, and what did it mean. "Something to do while I waited."

"I see." Mr. Henry sighed. "You know, we got to go to the police."

"Yeah." And I got in and he put Rache in the bed of the truck and got in too and we drove off into the dark.

It went about how you'd think after that. I mean, how you'd think once the cops found the gun in the backpack and connected me with the runaway kid up in Wyattville wanted for murder and kidnapping, trespassing and property damage, making fake emergency calls, and whatever else they could think up. Plus, it turns out the gun had my prints all over it, and it was the same gun that shot Big Joe. I admit I was surprised they put the cuffs on, me being a kid and all, and doing everything they told me, but they did. But like I said, everything else went how you'd think.

There was hearings and everybody wanted me to talk about what happened all the time but I didn't. For one thing, and the main thing, I wasn't in a real mood for talking, 'cause what the hell mattered without Rache there? Nothing, that's what. Absolutely nothing.

But besides that, it was like in the principal's office when he's already made up his mind, even if you didn't do what he thinks you did, so when he asks you for your side of the story don't waste your breath, right? He don't really care what you say, he just needs to check off on his little list that he asked for your side. He'll still suspend you from school for a week, but it'll be on him, 'cause he wanted to do it, not 'cause you played along like it was all fair, like you ever had a shot at getting off. So when all the lawyers and social workers and judges asked me their questions, I didn't bother.

I wasn't sleeping at all or even eating much and only going over in my head all that happened, my head going in circles all the time, especially at night I just laid with my eyes open until morning, just coming back 'round again and again to what I coulda shoulda done and Rache'd still be here, like the sun'd come up and we'd be in the tent together, her sleeping peaceful across from me.

That, and also I was wondering how long I'd be at Juvie until I could get out and go to the island and get the pictures back and thinking maybe the answer was never. But that's when Mizz Strickman had an idea. She said since I didn't want to talk about it I should write it all down to get it clear in my mind. And that was the first good idea anybody'd had for me. 'Cause Rache was gone but we still wasn't done yet. What she had wanted to do was just make things fair, like back in that principal's office if you actually had photographs of what happened and the principal would have to change his mind, no matter how much it galled him. And Mizz Strickman got me thinking, if I didn't have the pictures, maybe I could do it with words.

So I started writing and I knowed right off this couldn't be like an essay for school or whatever, it had to be a book so people would read it and know the truth. So when Mama and Robby come to visit I'll be able to look 'em in the eye 'cause they'll know I ain't really no murderer. Probably still not Granny or Aunt

Marnie, though, since I didn't do the one thing I was suppose to, and that's protect Rache. Of course there was a million things I could've done different and things wouldn't turn out like they did. The problem is, I can't actually figger what I would've done different if I'd had the chance, 'cause it all seemed like the best thing at the time.

The only thing that helps is when I'm writing this, when I'm working on it I eat and can even sleep some, so that's what I do, and 'cause Rache would've wanted the truth, that's what I put in. I mean, this book's been more work than I thought it would be, but now I'm done and here it is, probably the most truthful book you'll ever read, 'cause I wrote exactly what happened and didn't change a word, like I said I would at the start.

Maybe Sheriff Tate and Laban won't go to jail for it, or all the others who should. Probably it won't change a thing. But one thing about the truth, when you're telling it, the whole world can try to stare you down and you can stare right back without blinking. And even though Rache is gone, I think that's enough.

Maybe that's even how I like it. 'Cause one thing's for sure.

It's the whole damn world against J.T.

Just like usual.

Eileen Strickman, LCSW
New Hanover Co. Div.
of Juvenile Justice
138 N. 4th Street
Wilmington, NC 28401

Linda Kern
Public Defender's Office
320 Chestnut Street
Wilmington, NC 28401

October 16th, 1990

Dear Ms. Kern,

You asked me to keep you apprised on the progress of Jacob Thomas (J.T.) Honeycutt during his time at the Juvenile Justice Center. In view of that request, I am including in this mailing a copy of what he calls a manuscript, an account of his version of the events leading up to his arrest on July 5th.

J.T. has written this manuscript entirely by himself, although I typed it for him and have assisted him with some spelling, punctuation, and formatting. On the advice of Dr. Smith, I have not attempted to edit J.T.'s account or to steer his story in any way, although as you will see there are numerous details that are at the least implausible, and others that directly contradict the testimony of Sheriff Tate and the other evidence presented in connection with this case. Dr. Smith suggests this is J.T.'s way of reconciling himself to the two deaths, and is a necessary step to his eventual acceptance of responsibility.

Considering J.T.'s complete refusal to testify or even speak to anyone besides me since his arrest, including a refusal to see his family when they've come for visits, I think this manuscript shows he actually has a lot to say on his case. It also shows he's quite an intelligent and sensitive young man who's very disturbed by what happened, though perhaps not entirely aware of his own role in it. Dr. Smith is looking into whether he can use the manuscript as the basis for a psychiatric evaluation of J.T., which of course has proved impossible to conduct up until now.

I have to admit I was also disturbed, and perhaps curious, about some of the events described in the manuscript, and did a little research of my own into some of the people and places described. I know your office would have advised me against this; nevertheless, it may still be of interest for you to know what I've learned.

My attempt to locate the blind man, Jerry, proved to be a failure. As you might imagine, there are numerous convenience stores and small groceries offering bait along the Black River between Wilmington and Wyattville, but I was unable to locate one named Ed's, nor any in the vicinity of a

Family Dollar in the way J.T. described. I asked several employees and patrons of the stores I stopped at if they knew a blind man named Jerry, or any blind man who might occasionally stop at the store, but none of them did.

I had better luck finding Pastor Jim Holland at the New Life Salvation Bible Church in Alvieville, outside Fayetteville. However, he claimed to have never met J.T. or Rache, although when I explained a little about them he wondered if they were connected with a pair of break-ins last summer at the church when food was stolen from the pantry. He asked me to tell the kids that if they needed assistance in the future, the church offers a food bank for the needy, open on Thursdays. I asked to speak to youth pastor Brian, but he said Brian no longer worked there and he wasn't sure how to get in contact with him. I also asked him if it would be okay to contact his wife or if there were any church employees or parishioners I could speak to who might have seen something. He didn't believe so, and added that his family enjoyed their privacy. I left the matter alone.

Mr. Henry of course you are familiar with. He said he would do anything he could to help J.T., but that with his family's own involvement in the Shaquille White assault/coma case he didn't know what his help would be worth. I might point out that

J.T.'s account has him and Rache rather more entangled in that incident than had previously been known, and if accurate, may be useful for your office as evidence that the Henry twins' assault was not premeditated.

Finally, there's the matter of the pictures. Last weekend, a friend and I rented a speed boat. We searched all morning on the Cape Fear River and although we did spot a couple islets that looked like they might match J.T.'s, when we stopped to explore them we did not find the tent or any other sign the children had been there. But it has been more than three months since he claims to have camped on the river, and with all the recent rain from the remnants of Hurricane Klaus things might have been washed away.

Regardless of the veracity of the details, J.T.'s manuscript supplies at least some sort of outline of his actions between the murder of Joe Ammons and the kidnapping of Rachel Stevens on June 20th, and her death on July 4th. I hope your office might find the manuscript to be of some use in handling J.T.'s case.

Let me know if I can be of any further assistance.

Sincerely,

Eileen Strickman

Linda Kern
Public Defender's Office
320 Chestnut Street
Wilmington, NC 28401

Eileen Strickman, LCSW
New Hanover Co. Div. of Juvenile Justice
138 N. 4th Street
Wilmington, NC 28401

October 19th, 1990

Dear Ms. Strickman,

Thank you for your letter of October 16th and J.T.'s manuscript. It's longer than I expected but I will indeed review it in the next few days.

Please note I am forwarding to you via interoffice mail a small packet that arrived here for J.T. The return address says it is from Brian White. I will let you inspect it for appropriateness.

Sincerely,

Linda Kern.

Dear J.T.,

I see you on TV the other night! I so sorry to hear about Rache. I hope you doing okay.

For me, I live now with Pastor Brian. I think about you and Rache and decide is time for me to leave also. Pastor Jim not happy but cannot stop determined person.

Pastor Brian's house much better. I go to school and improve my English. You think my English getting better? He let me watch TV, walk to Alex's house. Alex is my new friend.

By the way, I find something on floor you leave behind, take it with me to Pastor Brian's house. I send it now. Pastor Brian say it called "photo negatives." I think it fall out your bag when you fight Ramon.

Hope you okay. I remember about you and Rache every day.

Your friend,

Hyun-Soo Kim

I'd like to thank all the people who helped me in the writing and production of this book: Angela Glascock, Pat Kallman, Anita Klein, Steve Moriarty, and the members of the Writers of Chantilly, who did much to improve this book with their comments and suggestions!

I hope you enjoyed reading *Jesus Bugs!* Because Amazon reviews are one of the main drivers of book sales, please consider leaving a brief but honest review on this book's Amazon page.

Sign up for my mailing list and receive a free short story!
nicholasbruner.com/contact

Look for
Mother Ink
The first book of an epic fantasy trilogy by Nicholas Bruner coming in Fall 2021!

www.ingramcontent.com/pod-product-compliance
Lightning Source LLC
Chambersburg PA
CBHW031700170626
46808CB00005B/1535

* 9 7 8 1 7 3 5 4 8 9 2 5 4 *